# SHAKE CITY

(A JACK MCCOUL CAPER BOOK 4)

DWIGHT HOLING

**Shake City**
(A Jack McCoul Caper)
Print Edition
Copyright 2017 by Dwight Holing
Published by Jackdaw Press
All Rights Reserved

ISBN: 978-0-9991468-0-4

For More Information, please visit dwightholing.com.

See how you can **Get a Free Book** at the end of this novel.

# 1

Sami Alfassi pinched a cigarette between his thumb and forefinger as he stood outside the door to his shoe store on Mission Street. He stared unblinkingly through a veil of smoke and by way of greeting said, "You are going to raise my rent."

Jack McCoul paused before entering the adjoining door that led to his office upstairs. "What makes you say that?"

Alfassi's eyes were hooded and his moustache as black as a brush's bristles. He wore a dark suit and white shirt buttoned at the neck with no tie. "You own the building. You can do as you please."

"That's not the way it works here. There's still three years on your lease."

Alfassi blocked him with a wave of his cigarette. "Rules change."

It was a bright spring morning without a hint of fog and Jack had strolled to work from his loft down by the Giants ballpark. A colorful parade of vehicles jammed the street and pedestrians crowded the sidewalks. Jack could taste Salvadorian *pupusas* and

Levantine *baba ghanoush* in the air as a potluck of smells wafted from dozens of restaurants.

The shopkeeper took a drag before continuing. "I had a house in Aleppo. One day a government man came and said for every ten bricks, President Assad owned nine and I had to pay him. Later the military bombed the city. My house? A heap of rubble, nothing more. I went to the government man and said, 'Tell the president we need to rebuild. I will pay for my one brick and he for his nine.' " He made a spitting sound without spitting. "Do you know what he did?"

"I can guess, but this isn't Syria. Your lease is solid."

Alfassi let the smoke trail from both nostrils. His nose had been broken. A scar split his left eyebrow, leaving one side higher.

"All the shops here, the rent, it keeps going up." He pointed to a hole-in-the-wall storefront next door. A sign advertised check cashing and money transfer services in English, Spanish, and Tagalog. "The owner, his name is Garza. They are raising his rent 400 percent. He refuses to pay. The restaurant up the street, the one that sells Mexican dishes, they are being evicted. They were not given a choice to pay more."

"But I'm not doing that," Jack said.

"How are we to stay in business with this happening? And the apartments, it is the same. How are we to live with this happening?"

"That's a question for the City."

"Ah, the government." The shopkeeper made the spitting sound again. "People have gone to speak with these officials. Garza did. He told them what is taking place, described the terrorizing by the building's owner, but—"

"What do you mean *terrorizing*?"

"Some people get knocks on their apartment doors in the middle of the night. Phone calls with threats. Letters with threats in their mailboxes. Men come into stores and break things. Get out, they say, get out or get hurt." The cigarette's ember reflected in his eyes. "Garza? After he made his complaint, his storefront was painted with obscenities, his locks filled with glue. His landlord would not pay to repair it."

"Did he tell the cops?"

Alfassi shrugged. "Most people remember the police from where they came from. I could tell you stories about my country."

"Look, you don't have to worry about your rent. And no one's going to knock on your door in the middle of the night or mess with your merchandise. I'm lucky to have you as a tenant. You're a smart businessman. Your store is always crowded."

"Then why do not you buy shoes from me?"

Jack glanced at Alfassi's storefront window. "DiscOunt" was spelled in bright red press-on letters. "Okay, my next pair. You got my word." He moved to get past him.

"And shoes for your wife also? I sell only the latest ladies fashions. Special deal for you."

"Why not? I'll ask Katie to stop by."

"And for your children also. The little girl and boy."

"Zita, sure. But Harry? He doesn't even walk yet."

Alfassi wetted his fingertips and extinguished what remained of the cigarette. He field stripped the butt and cupped it in his palm. Three fingernails were missing and his pinky formed a backwards 7.

"When we fled Aleppo we walked over the border, across Turkey, and all the way to Serbia. My children did not have shoes."

Jack sucked his teeth. "Okay, four pairs it is. Like I said, you're a smart businessman."

The shopkeeper stuck the remains of the cigarette in his jacket pocket and lit a new one. "*Inshallah*, you do not change the rules." He turned his hawk-like gaze on the feet of passersby and called out the specials he had inside.

JACK'S OFFICE was right above the shoe store. He'd positioned his desk so he could watch the nonstop action on the street below. The view was a tonic for having given up the life and going legit.

Once upon a time Mission Street was a two-mile long track made of wooden planks that led from the Spanish *ranchos* to Yerba Buena, the waterfront settlement that grew up to become San Francisco. Eventually the street became the city's cultural artery as the district that bore its name welcomed wave after wave of working-class immigrants. First it was Irish families like Jack's, and then Germans and Polish. Later Mexicans, Central Americans, and Asians moved in. But the latest surge of arrivals was unlike any other, and it was disrupting the Mission as surely as the companies that employed them were disrupting taxis, hotels, and dating.

A flurry of construction was the most obvious sign of changing times. Whenever a familiar landmark was demolished and a new stack of cookie-cutter apartments rose in its place, Jack would think of his mother when her hair started falling out from the chemo. She bought a cheap synthetic wig, but it never lost its sparkly shine and plastic smell. Jack threw it away the night she died so she wouldn't have to spend eternity with the damn thing.

His own entrance into the world of commercial real estate left him open to accusations like the kind Sami Alfassi lobbed, but cashing in on the development boom had never been his goal. Jack simply needed a place to stash some cash after a big score and was following the golden rule for any investment: buy what you know, run from what you don't.

Managing property in his childhood neighborhood came with benefits. It bestowed a patina of legitimacy after so many years working on the wrong side of the law as a con artist, and the office provided balance to a home life that had been disrupted as surely as the old economy. A three-year-old and a newborn had arrived within a couple of weeks of each other the previous fall and Jack had been scrambling to adapt ever since. Learning to take care of kids was one thing, learning to give up the life was another.

Jack turned his attention to his laptop's screen and prowled through a list of unread e-mail. He was studying a bid to paint the building when a young woman wearing enormous gold hoop earrings and matching platform shoes opened the door.

"I have rent but sorry I one hundred dollar short. I make it up tonight with tips and put under door, okay?" Valentine Song pulled a handful of bills from a large purse made of faux leopard skin.

"Don't sweat it. I know you're good for it," he said.

"You the best."

Valentine Song was a stage name, a reconfiguration of Vitchuda Songprawati. The Thai *émigré* lived in a studio apartment that was the across-the-hall twin to Jack's office. There were four other apartments on the floor.

Jack leaned back. "How's everything going?"

"Busy, busy. I have two jobs now. That and go to City College. I study English and computer coding."

"The American Dream. You still dancing at the Gold Rush Club?" It was a strip joint that fostered its own patina of legitimacy by having a Financial District street address and bouncers dressed in Zegna suits.

"Oh yes, I work buffet lunch crowd. Five-dollar cover buy customer all-they-can-eat and all-they-can-watch. Best deal in town and fried chicken breast and thigh not bad either." Her smile lit up the room.

"Sounds like a Yelp review."

"Oh yes, the owner make us girls say to customers. He think it funny."

"Figures."

"You know what I think funny? Construction workers tip better than bankers or men from convention center."

"Hard hats appreciate hard work."

"Oh yes, I think you right."

"What's your new job?"

"I working four nights a week at Double Dice now."

"Serving or mixing?"

"Serving. Tips always less when you stand behind bar."

"You must be socking it away. Two jobs and one of them doesn't cost you bus fare, the Double Dice being right across the street here."

"Oh yes, it very convenience." She paused. "That right?"

"Close enough."

"Double Dice pay enough for school now."

In the old days the Double Dice had a reputation as one of the toughest dive bars in the Mission. It specialized in beers and shots, nine ball, and brawls. A sign behind the bar warned "No crying, no Dodgers."

"I'll have to drop by," Jack said. "I haven't been there since DD Mitchell took over from his old man and gave it a facelift."

"Oh yes, very hip now. Many cocktails with funny names. Mission Mule Shoe. San Francisco Sloe Gin Slush. They call signature drinks. Everyone at table always order something different. The menu so big it is in a book."

"Since when did reading become a requirement for drinking?"

Valentine cocked her head. "I not understand."

"Never mind. You like working there?"

Now her head dipped. Her long black hair was tied in an over-the-shoulder fall that hung nearly to her waist. A streak of purple ran through it. She looked back up. "It okay, I guess."

"You don't sound so sure. The way you said it. *Okay*."

"There always customer not so friendly by being too friendly. You know what I mean?"

"If the guy doesn't get the message, tell DD to eighty-six him."

"What eighty-six mean?"

"Bar him from the bar."

"Oh yes, DD not do that. He say customer always right."

"Who's the customer?"

Valentine pursed her lips. "He nobody. I go dance now at Gold Rush. I put rest of money under door tonight. Bye-bye, Jack. You the best. I see you later, okay?"

And with that she was gone, leaving behind a wad of cash and a lingering scent of lemongrass and jasmine.

Hark's custom paint and body shop was a few minutes' walk from Jack's office. The big man's rolling billboard—a '64 Chevy Impala lowrider—was parked out front. The doors to the building's bays were open and the whine of an orbital buffer competed with guitar riffs from Los Lobos' *Gates of Gold* album.

A thin teenager wearing a respirator and hair net was polishing a newly painted sapphire '72 Caprice as Hark coached him.

"Remember, *chico*, it's all in the touch. Treat her like a woman. You got to see the soul beneath the surface before you make any moves. That's it. Now you got it. And never forget to always give her the respect she deserves."

Hark wore an untucked, long-sleeved flannel shirt and a bandana tied low on his forehead. When he spotted Jack, his wide grin made the dark blue gothic letters that spelled out *Herald* on his neck ripple.

"Hey, Vinny, shut it down. I got someone I want you to meet. This is my *'mano*, Jack McCoul. Jack, say hello to Vinny Vargas."

The teen said something, but it was muffled by the respirator.

Hark pointed at it. "Lose the mask."

Vinny pulled it down and stuck out his fist. "*¿Qué onda,* man?"

Jack returned the bump. "What's up?"

The teen followed with a choreographed series of slaps and slides. Jack kept up. Vinny raised a brow in admiration. "*Chido.*"

"Yeah, Jack's cool, all right," Hark said. "Enough small talk. Back to work." He hooked a thumb toward the front showroom.

Jack followed. "Where did you find him?"

"I caught him tagging my wall. He had a cannon of Krylon in each hand. One orange, one black."

"At least he was flying the Giants' colors. So instead of giving him a smack you gave him a job."

"Hey, kid has talent as a sprayer, no doubt about it. I got him detailing, masking, and so on. Let him work up to the booth."

"You adding guidance counselor to your résumé now? Gangbanger, decorated war vet, business owner."

Hark's expression was half scowl, half smile. "I sure coulda used somebody looking out for me when I was coming up. Woulda saved some hard times and even harder lessons."

"That's one way to describe a jolt in juvie."

"You know what I mean. Someone pointing out the bumps in the road that cost more than blood and bone if you hit 'em."

"We both missed out on the TV dad role model, that's for sure."

"Roger that," Hark said.

Jack's father was a fireman who beat his wife and kids but didn't beat the odds when a burning roof came tumbling down. Hark's was anybody's guess.

The newest issue of *Lowrider Magazine* was on the counter.

Jack picked it up. The center foldout unfurled. It was an emerald Monte Carlo caught in midhop. The front tires were three feet off the ground.

"Vinny living on the streets or does he got a home?" he asked.

"He's been couch surfing so I'm letting him crib here. It's a good thing too. He's keeping an eye on the place after hours. Like a night watchman."

"He bombs your building and then you pay him to guard against other night writers? Reminds me of the Wallinskis. Those brothers who lived over in the Excelsior. Owned a burglar alarm company and went around breaking into places to create themselves a steady supply of new customers."

Hark's biceps stretched the flannel sleeves of his shirt as he crossed his arms. "Yeah, I remember those *güeros*. But I mean the shit going down right now. Mission's always been a tough 'hood, but the techie and Tesla set ain't exactly brought an upgrade when it comes to law and order. And I'm not talking about the usual street hustles and smash and grabs."

Jack said, "My tenant Sami Alfassi was just telling me. Shopkeepers getting intimidated to make way for folks with deeper pockets and stock options."

"If you mean intimidated being a dude in a suit serving an eviction notice, it's way past that, *vato*. More like goon squads with studded gloves and sledgehammers. This keeps up, someone's going get more than hurt."

Jack put the magazine back on the counter. "I told Alfassi the renters should take it down to city hall."

"Sure, but you know where that's going go. Maybe a blueribbon commission to study it until after the election that's coming up. Meanwhile people going be trading their cars for shopping carts and setting up house in cardboard boxes."

"I came over to take you to lunch, not talk politics."

Hark grinned. "If you're buying, I'm eating. Let's ride."

THEY WALKED, not drove, because Abuelita's Restaurant was right around the corner. Hark's grandmother ran the restaurant with a cast iron griddle and a gold-toothed smile. Jack had spent more time there than he did his own home during high school, mainly to keep out of the way of his father's flying fists and bottles. The restaurant was one of many that lined Valencia Street, but it had changed little since its founding and the loyal fans who craved *frijoles* cooked with lard and handmade tortillas wouldn't have it any other way.

Hark went behind the bar to retrieve a couple of cold ones while Jack headed straight to the kitchen.

"*Hola, Abuelita.* Did Katie drop off a little helper today?"

The old woman smiled and pointed her chin over her shoulder. Jack tiptoed around her.

"Hey, little girl."

Zita was standing on a chair at the counter. She had flour on her nose and a stain on her apron.

"*Hola*, Jack," she said.

He kissed the top of her head. She had black Irish hair like his, but sapphire eyes like her late mother.

"What are you making?" he asked.

"*Empanadas.*"

Jack said to the old lady, "Is she teaching you Argentine cooking now?"

Her gold fillings flashed. "*Su hija es muy inteligente.*"

"Thanks for looking after her. I'm going to grab some lunch with Hark and then take her home."

"*No problema. Me encanta tener su aquí.*"

"She loves being here too." He reached over and took a pinch of the dough his daughter was patting out and tasted it. "Hmm, very good. You want to eat lunch with me?"

She shook her head. "No. I have to finish these. *Le promotí a la Abuelita.*"

"Okay, a promise is a promise. Let's race. I'll go eat and you keep cooking. We'll see who finishes first."

Zita laughed and started pounding the dough with both palms as fast as she could.

Hark was already working on a basket of chips and freshly made *pico de gallo* when Jack joined him.

"Expect a change in the menu," Jack said as he pushed a wedge of lime down the neck of a bottle of Pacifico. "Zita's teaching your grandma how to make a new dish."

Hark picked up his beer. "She feels right at home here. My *abuelita* in the kitchen, all the Spanish, it must remind her of the *estancia* in Argentina we found her at."

They looked at each other over the bottles, their eyes saying it all, each remembering what had gone down there.

Hark broke the recollection. "I can't believe how fast she's learned English."

"Katie says kids pick up languages a lot easier than adults do. The younger, the quicker."

"Their heads ain't filled up from TV and stuff. She start calling you daddy yet?"

Jack waved the beer bottle. "She can call me whatever she wants."

They didn't bother with a menu. It wouldn't've mattered anyway. Hark's grandmother served them what she wanted. It was always good and nothing was ever left on the plate. Today it was *carne asada con mole negro*. A grilled *poblano* stuffed with shrimp accompanied the main.

Jack said, "You ever wonder what your father's name was?"

"Never," the big man said. "As far as I'm concerned, it was *hijo de puta*, he not owning up. If he had any respect at all, my mama wouldn't have had to leave me with my *abuelita* and go down to L.A. to find work."

It was as if Los Angeles had swallowed Hark's mother whole. When he was fourteen he stole a car and drove down to look for her. He repeated the search every year on his birthday, except for when he was stationed in Afghanistan. Jack let the matter drop. He'd only asked because he was still trying to work it out himself what it meant to be a dad.

They finished eating. Jack mopped up the last of the *mole* with a perfectly freckled flour tortilla and left Hark at the table as he walked back to the kitchen to round up Zita. He was leading her from the kitchen when the restaurant's front door banged opened and two men entered.

Hark jumped up as soon as he saw them. "You must have Alzheimer's," he growled at the shorter man as he blocked the pair's entrance. "I told you two times too many already you don't show up here without sending a twenty-four hour notice first. Now beat it."

Jack recognized Frank Penny Jr. He was a former schoolmate at St. Joseph's. His father owned property in the Mission District and Penny Jr. was always throwing his weight around. His hair shined with product, and he wore a three-quarter length duster once made fashionable by Australian movie stars.

"No need for bad manners, Geraldo." Penny Jr. smirked at Hark. "This is simply a courtesy call. Your grandmother never returned the form acknowledging receipt of the terms of her new lease. Failure to sign is cause to terminate." He paused. "The lease, that is."

Hark clenched his fists and took a step closer. The second man countered wordlessly by moving between Hark and Penny

Jr. He put his right hand into the pocket of his Oakland Raiders team jacket. Hark didn't blink. He lifted the tail of his flannel to reveal the butt of a GI-issued Beretta M9 tucked in his waistband. Years spent in a Mission District gang followed by two tours of duty at a forward operating base made for habits that died hard.

Jack whisked Zita behind him. "How you doing, Frankie? Been a while."

Penny Jr. looked past Hark. "Oh, Jack. I didn't see you there. And it's Frank now."

"Okay, Frank Now. Since when did your old man have a stake in this building?"

"Turns out the previous owner was over-leveraged. My father and I acquired the portfolio which included this storefront and..." His smile showed off his daddy's considerable investment in orthodontia. "Most of the block."

"Not all," Hark said. "I own my body shop."

"It's *we*. My father and me are partners. And it's only a matter of time before we do." Penny Jr. gave an exaggerated sigh. "You're like all the other shopkeepers who can't see the big picture. Barrios are dinosaurs. You either get out of the way of progress or get run over by it. By the way, are you sure you have all your environmental permits in order?"

Jack spoke before Hark could react. "Okay, Frankie. Hark and I'll help his grandmother look for the form. We find it, we'll be sure to let you know. That is, after her lawyer takes a look to make sure all the i's are dotted."

"I told you, it's Frank. Who's her lawyer?"

"Cicero Broadshank."

"No way she can afford him. Besides, he only does criminal defense."

"He's my lawyer and what you're doing is criminal."

"I'll tell my father and we'll see who has the best legal team."

Jack laughed. "Same old Frankie. Remember back at Saint Joe's? Your old man had to stuff a fat envelope into the collection plate every Sunday just so Father Bernardus would add your name to the lineup. You couldn't catch, couldn't throw, couldn't run, couldn't hit. Baseball's a simple game but somehow you managed to screw it up." He glanced at the man in the black and silver team jacket and then said, "What, daddy buy you a playmate too?"

The man curled his lip. A blond goatee framed it. "I heard of you, McCoul. From where I stand, I don't see what the big deal is."

"Maybe I've heard of you too. What's your name?"

"Ricky Udo." He said it like he practiced saying it in the mirror every morning.

Jack turned to Hark. "Rings a bell. Doesn't one of those food trucks down on Division sell bowls of udo?"

Hark laughed.

"Keep it up," Udo said. "We'll see who laughs last."

Jack said, "See you around, Frankie. Make sure to say hi to your dad for me."

Penny Jr. started to say something, but thought better. He spun on the heels of his new Wellingtons and pushed through the door. Ricky Udo shot another curled lip before following him out.

Hark said, "What's with Frankie's get up? He some kinda cowboy now?"

"The closest he's ever gotten to riding a wild brumby is on his living room couch in front of a widescreen. Frank Sr. must've hired Udo as a babysitter to keep Junior from soiling his fancy duds."

"See, this is exactly the kinda shit what I was telling you

about. All the money flowing into the Mission is making even the little *pendejos* think they're big *pendejos*."

Zita stepped out from behind Jack. "Ooh, Uncle Hark said a naughty word. *Pendejo* means asshole."

Jack shrugged at Hark. "I told you kids pick up languages fast."

**E**vening was seeping into San Francisco. The sky slowly lost any vestiges of blue while the bay darkened more quickly as if readying itself to accept the reflection of lights from the bridges that spanned it. Bartenders cranked up the music and restaurant crews picked up the pace in preparation for the after-work crowd.

Miles Davis was blowing cool as Jack watched the light change from his loft overlooking Anchorage Nine, a deepwater mooring just past the ballpark's right field wall. The hum of hawsers from the tankers straining against the tide made the building's windows vibrate. He'd remodeled the space to create a second bedroom and Zita was in there now devouring books. She was already reading at the third-grade level despite being too young for kindergarten.

The front door opened and Katie swooped in. "That better be my glass of wine you're holding because you're going to have your hands full in a second."

Jack traded the glass of Lambrusco for the sleeping nine-month-old. He hoisted Harry up and down a couple of times as if judging the weight of a piglet at a country fair. "You sure you didn't grab a sack of dumbbells by mistake?"

"Pretty sure," she said with a laugh.

Katie owned a string of gyms that were part of a growing empire aimed at promoting women's health, wellness, and fashion. "Feel Great, Be Great" was her company's slogan.

Jack held the baby out at arm's distance. "Look at him. He's turning into a gym rat."

"What can I say? Your son loves baby yoga."

"How's that working out, offering free childcare for your members? Your members who don't pay a membership fee because you don't charge one, I might add."

"Don't knock it. It's a huge advantage for us. I'm looking at opening a new location."

That surprised him. Katie already had five, and he thought she was holding off on expansion while they got used to child-rearing. All he could think of saying was *where*.

"Another one right here in the city. My first choice is the Mission." Her smile widened. "Know any place with reasonable rent?"

"Even if I had a vacancy, I don't think you could afford it," he volleyed.

She gave him a coy look. "Maybe we could work out a special arrangement."

"How about I put this little porker down and we start working on that arrangement right now?"

"Sure," she said. "After you change his diaper first."

"Mood killer," he said.

∼

"Did you feel that?" Katie said.

"I sure did," Jack said sleepily. He patted her hip.

They were lying in bed and she was tucked up against him, her head resting in the crook of his arm. The lights were down low, the windows open. Car alarms started chirping in the distance. Burglar alarms too.

"I meant the earth move," she said.

"You're welcome."

Katie elbowed him. "Not that. The building. I felt it shake. I think there was an earthquake."

Jack opened his eyes. "Really? Must have been sizeable to rattle this old hulk. The walls are two feet thick."

"Check the web and see if I'm right."

Jack rolled over and reached for his phone. Tremors were nothing new and there hadn't been a big one since the Loma Prieta, but he kept an updated quake app that mirrored the US Geological Survey's seismic activity site. He tapped the icon and the screen filled with an outlined map of the world and then red lines depicting major earthquake faults snaked across the display. Dots of varying sizes appeared next. A text box on the side listed earthquakes with a magnitude of 2.5 or higher in the past twenty-four hours. He zoomed in on California.

"Just a couple of small ones down in Parkfield, but that place is always shaking. It's probably because of all the oil drilling. Like fracking is doing to Oklahoma."

"I sure felt something," Katie said and swung her legs out of bed. "I'm going to check on the kids."

Jack propped himself on the pillows and hit refresh. The list of quakes updated and the newest log showed a 3.1 centered on the Hayward Fault across the bay. When Katie returned he said, "You were right but I doubt it did anything more than tilt a few pictures on some walls."

She tapped the corner of her eye. "Woman's sixth sense."

Jack pointed the phone toward the second bedroom. "All quiet on the western front?"

"I know I shouldn't worry, but I do. Dr. Wang says Zita is doing really well. You know, adapting to her new environment and all, but there's always a risk something could trigger PTSD."

Jack sometimes wondered the same thing about himself. Zita hadn't seen her mother die, but Jack had, and as much as he tried to bury the memory, the scene had a way of resurfacing at the most inconvenient times. It always brought a feeling that he could've done more to have saved her. When he started thinking like that, he started wondering if maybe he was losing his edge, that the headlong rush into domesticity had side effects he'd never imagined.

Katie's gaze signaled she knew what he was thinking. She slipped back under the comforter, put her hand on Jack's chest, and draped a leg over his.

"Are you still looking at the earthquake app?" she asked.

"Yeah, but there's not much info since it was such a small shake."

"Maybe we ought to get a little seismic ourselves."

He raised an eyebrow. "Again?"

"Earthquakes aren't the only thing that come in swarms."

———

## 4

Traffic on Mission Street was snarled despite the early hour. Blue and red flashes from emergency vehicles up ahead fractured the fading sunrise. Jack hung a quick left, double-parked the Prius, and jogged toward his office. A uniformed cop halted him at the corner.

"Get back," he ordered. "No gawkers."

"I own the building where they found the body," Jack said.

"So what?"

"So, the investigators are going to want to talk to me. You want to explain to them why you interfered?"

They locked eyes. The cop didn't shed his hard stare, but he finally nodded and Jack didn't wait for a second opinion.

Yellow tape had already been strung across the sidewalk so he juked into the street and made an end around the parked cars. He reached the front of his building, but no cops were stationed there. They were next door guarding the entrance to the check cashing and money transfer shop. Sami Alfassi stood in the doorway of the shoe store. He was smoking a cigarette.

Jack said, "I heard it on the radio. They said the block, not the street number. I thought it might be one of my tenants. You know what happened?"

"Garza was murdered." The Syrian said it so matter-of-factly he may as well have been describing what he had for dinner.

"Are you sure?"

"More than one bullet is rarely a suicide."

"The cops tell you this?"

Alfassi picked a flake of tobacco from his lip. "They told each other. They assumed I do not speak English."

"But you do."

"I was a school teacher before I came to America. Now I sell shoes. The way of the world, no?"

Jack said, "You know who called it in?"

"A customer. Garza opens at 5:00 a.m. and does not close until midnight. People need to wire money back home where it is already tomorrow. She is still in there. I assume she is being questioned." He shoved his hand with the missing fingernails and pinkie bent like a backwards 7 into his suit jacket pocket as he spoke.

The pair of uniformed cops guarding Garza's shop suddenly marched into the middle of the street and began clearing the traffic jam. A black Crown Victoria with emergency lights flashing behind the front grill made its way through. It stopped and Lieutenant Terrence Dolan exited. The stripes on his rep tie reminded Jack of dawn and fog. The detective paused to pull on a pair of paper booties before entering the check cashing store.

Alfassi exhaled smoke through his nostrils. "Ah, the government man."

"He's a cop. A detective with SFPD Robbery Homicide."

"The same thing as the government, is it not? Do you know him?"

"Since we were kids."

Jack didn't add they were rivals, and not only because they'd spent their lives on opposite sides of the law. The cop once planned to marry Katie. He still blamed Jack for stealing her heart.

Alfassi took another drag on his cigarette. "You say he is with Robbery *and* Homicide? That is good because here the two are as connected as a camel to its hump. First the theft when they raised his rent and now the murder when he refused to pay."

"Maybe, maybe not. You ever heard of Willie Sutton?"

"Does he live here in the neighborhood?"

"He was a bank robber. When they asked him why he robbed banks, he said that's where the money is. People paid cash to Garza to make wire transfers and he cashed their checks. Wouldn't be the first time a shopkeeper got shot during a holdup."

"Perhaps, but I believe your friend from the government would be wise to investigate the people who own the building first." He blew smoke out his broken nose.

Jack stared at Garza's shop. The wall still showed traces of spray painted obscenities. "You said the customer who discovered the body was a *she*. Know her?"

"As do you. It is your tenant, Miss Song."

The shopkeeper extinguished the cigarette with his fingertips and placed the butt in his pocket before returning to his shoe store and closing the door.

The cops were still in the street directing traffic so Jack walked over to Garza's and looked inside. The layout was a poor man's bank with a beat-up counter separating a cramped lobby and a dingy office decorated with a calendar advertising an insurance company and old travel posters. A crime scene investigator was hovering over a cluttered desk, dusting it for fingerprints. The computer screen and keyboard already sported blotches the color of bruises. So did the vintage adding machine. A clunky fax machine stood on a table with thick wooden legs. Beneath the table was a green safe the size of a mini refrigerator. Its door was open, the shelves were bare.

Valentine Song sat in the corner. She hugged herself and the usual sunny smile was nowhere to be seen. The detective stood next to her. He held a black notebook and pen. A holster clipped to his belt marred the drape of his suit jacket.

She waved at Jack. "Oh yes, hi Jack. Please help. Tell policeman officer I live with you. You the best."

The homicide cop turned and surprise flickered in his eyes.

Jack said, "Valentine means she lives in one of my apartments. I own the building next door. How you doing, Terry?"

The stripper started nodding. "Oh yes, what I told you. See? Jack know I hard worker. Go to school also. I learning English. He the best."

The detective jabbed his notebook at Jack. "Don't take another step. You're contaminating the scene."

"How about a step backward?"

The cop shook his head tiredly. "Same old Jack."

"Okay, I'm leaving. One question first."

"What is it?"

"What did you have for breakfast?"

"What's that have to do with anything?"

"Must have been pretty tasty to keep you at the table. I heard about this on the radio and got here long before you did."

Anger darkened Terry's face, but before he could respond, a second crime scene investigator wearing a UV head lamp stood up from where she'd been crouched behind the counter. She held a plastic evidence bag in one hand and a pair of forceps in the other.

"I've done as much as I can with the vic, LT. We'll find out more once we get him in the sink, but two to the heart is going to be your cause. The third to the temple?" She made a face of disgust. "You want me to call in the body snatchers?"

The detective nodded curtly. Then he said to Valentine Song, "You're free to go. If we need anything, we know where to find you."

"Oh yes, I go now." When she reached Jack, she touched his arm. "Not nice way to start the day. Poor Mr. Garza. He the best. I feel sad."

"Maybe you should go home and take it easy."

"Oh yes, but I cannot. I get fired. I go now and get ready to dance at Gold Rush Club. See you later, Jack."

She hurried down the sidewalk. A TV news van pulled in behind the Crown Vic. A woman in the passenger seat checked her makeup in the visor's mirror. A white sedan waved in by one of the uniformed cops parked right behind. The door bore an official seal.

"Better straighten your tie," Jack said to Terry. "Your number one fan just showed up followed by the man who would be king."

DAYLIGHT BRIGHTENED and Jack stood among the gathering crowd. The camera crew shot establishing footage as reporter Shauna Rhames and her producer huddled outside the door to Garza's shop. When the homicide detective finally emerged, the producer signaled ready, set, go with a twirl of her finger.

"We're going live in five with breaking," she said. "Make it good, Shauna baby, and you'll get the lead-in for prime and late night too."

Rhames held the microphone and fixed her brown eyes on the camera's lens. "We're here on Mission Street where a brutal murder took place inside a check cashing store. Sources say multiple gunshots were fired. Residents are terrified. Joining me is Lieutenant Terrence Dolan of the Homicide Department."

Terry was plenty seasoned when it came to handling the media, whether it was holding off a scrum of reporters on the street or leading a press conference at city hall. Jack figured it was one of the reasons the cop always wore a pressed suit and carefully knotted tie. His ambition to rise from cop to chief was no secret. When Shauna Rhames shoved the mike in his face, he didn't blink.

"What can you tell us?" she asked.

"At 5:22 this morning 911 received a call about an unresponsive male. Officers were dispatched and determined the subject was deceased under suspicious circumstances. An investigation is now underway."

The producer had positioned herself so she could maintain eye contact with her reporter. She mouthed, "Boring."

Rhames switched to a *60 Minutes* meets *Access Hollywood* tone. "Sources say the victim was shot multiple times. Can you confirm that?"

"The coroner will need to conduct an autopsy to make an official determination of cause of death."

"And the name of the victim?"

"Identification is being withheld pending notification of next of kin."

"Was this a robbery or something else?"

"We are still in the very early stage of the investigation," Terry replied evenly.

The producer steepled her palms, rested her head on them, and mimed snoring.

Rhames shoved her microphone at the detective's teeth. "And what are you doing to apprehend the murderer?"

"We do not comment on specific tactics, but what I can say is we invite anyone who may have seen or heard anything to contact the police department."

Rhames shot the camera a sideways look and sighed. "So,

what you're saying is a man has been murdered, a dangerous killer or killers are on the loose, and the only thing the police are doing is asking people to call in leads?"

Terry ignored the bait. "The San Francisco Police Department is doing what it is sworn to do. Keeping the public safe. Period."

The producer directed the camera operator to zoom in on Rhames and cut the detective from the frame. The reporter raised her shoulders inside her red jacket and stuck out her chin.

"There you have it. Another murder in San Francisco and the public is left with more questions than answers. Reporting live for Action News, this is—"

"I may have some answers." It was the man who'd arrived in the white car with the seal on the door.

The camera swung toward him and then back to the reporter.

"Supervisor Erick Berlin has just arrived," Rhames said. "Let's see if I can get him to talk."

She strode purposely toward him, the camera following as if tracking a lioness chasing down dinner.

Erick Berlin not only showed no fear of the approaching camera, he appeared to have put on TV makeup. He wore a stylish open collared shirt beneath a dark blazer. He'd only been in town a few years, but already had become a media darling. Young, glib and telegenic, he'd parlayed a position as a charismatic community organizer into a seat on the powerful eleven-member board of supervisors, the legislative branch of the City and County of San Francisco. Now he was running for mayor.

"Supervisor, the police seem to have no answers to this horrible crime. What can you tell us?"

"It's a terrible tragedy, Shauna. And also a painful reminder that San Francisco policing is woefully inadequate. Families deserve to feel safe in their homes, schools, and workplaces. Especially vulnerable are low income families and the elderly. Incidents like this make me think of my own grandmother. She was a hardworking woman who raised me and taught me so much. Senior citizens like her deserve better."

"What would you do to protect people?"

"It starts with police walking beats not driving streets. Our city is crying out for community policing."

"Is that something you'll work toward if elected mayor?"

"Yes, but community policing is only part of the solution. Another problem crying out for attention are the derelict buildings that have been allowed to fester as havens for drug addicts and criminals. It's no wonder we have murders like the tragedy here today. We must take practical but aggressive actions to clean up problem areas like Mission Street."

"Do you have a specific plan for doing that?"

"We need to remove the political and economic harnesses that have held back development. We need to build affordable new housing for low income families and the elderly and transform outdated retail stores into robust consumer outposts for the new economy. Progress like that will create jobs and push out crime."

"Making the world safe one trendy restaurant and electronic gizmo store at a time," Jack muttered.

Berlin kept going. "We also need to ensure that every structure in this city is seismically sound. We had an earthquake last night. Fortunately, it wasn't a big one, but we all know it's only a matter of time. That's why I'm going to look into how we can toughen our seismic safety standards. Families must be kept safe."

The camera zoomed in on the reporter. "There you have it, an elected official who has more answers than the police. For Action News, this is Shauna Rhames."

## 5

The regulars were drinking breakfast at The Pier Inn, a white clapboard institution perched over the water in the shadow of the Bay Bridge. Wonder Boy manned the bar.

"S-s-salutations," he said. "The usual?"

Jack settled on a stool. "Hold the Jameson. I've been up since dawn and my day's looking to get even longer."

The bartender filled a thick heavy ceramic mug with coffee that was even thicker and heavier. "I s-s-see you've already been to Mission S-S-Street."

"Is there anything you don't know?"

Wonder didn't answer and Jack didn't expect him to. He was much too modest for that. The savant's network of snitches, gossips, and insiders had no equal.

Jack asked him what the word on the street was about what had gone down.

"The police s-s-seem to be focused on a robbery. The victim is Pietro Garza. He comes from an old S-S-San Francisco family. The grandfather was a s-s-sardine fisherman. When the fishery collapsed in the 1950s, they went into the s-s-storefront money business."

Jack blew on the coffee. "Better watch out. You've got new competition. Erick Berlin acts as if he's more wired into the community than you are. He got to the scene in time to grab plenty of spotlight."

Wonder wiped the bar with a white towel. He maintained it like an altar, believing the wood was a plank from Sir Francis Drake's ship. "I'm sure he heard as s-s-soon as S-S-Shauna Rhames did. You do know they are s-s-sleeping together."

"I've been too busy changing diapers, but it figures. They drove up in separate vehicles but were tailgating up Mission. Terry Dolan caught the case and they were finishing each other's sentences while they tag teamed, pinning him to the mat."

"The s-s-supervisor has made community policing a plank in his campaign platform."

"Too bad for Terry. Berlin needs someone to step on to give him a leg up on his rivals. A cop laboring to keep up with a growing homicide rate is just the ticket."

"S-s-six to five. Those are the odds Berlin will beat the incumbent. If you want to place a wager, I know someone."

"There's nobody you don't know, but I'll pass. I work too hard for my money now. Being a dad? It makes running a *Spanish Prisoner* seem like a walk in the park. I'm starting to think if I ran into an old mark seeking payback for a takedown, I'd wet my pants." He mimed shaking.

Wonder Boy didn't laugh. He never did. He moved down the bar to lubricate another patron. Jack checked his phone for e-mails. Most was spam from realtors trying to get him to list his buildings or buy another. One was from Frank Penny & Son Real Estate. It stated they had a well-qualified buyer with a large equity position who was in a 1031 exchange and needed to close on a replacement property right away or forfeit the capital gains tax deferral. A highlighted line caught Jack's eye: *Lock in profits now before costly new seismic safety standards become law.*

Wonder Boy returned. Jack said, "Did you feel an earthquake last night?"

"Three."

"My app only logged the 3.1."

"There were two s-s-smaller aftershocks. Each measured under 2.4."

"And you could feel them?" He knew better than to ask what kind of building Wonder Boy lived in or in which neighborhood. The sibilant-challenged savant guarded his privacy with the same tenacity he shielded the identity of his sources.

"My s-s-seismometer has an audio alarm."

"Of course it does. Three that close together, what, they're building up to the big one?"

Wonder's eyes fixated on the bar. "It is difficult to s-s-say, but there are s-s-several million earthquakes every year. Most are too s-s-small to be felt, but fifteen hundred or s-s-so are greater than a five magnitude. Those are large enough to cause s-s-significant damage."

"Magnitude meaning the Richter Scale."

"S-s-scientists use an updated measurement s-s-system now s-s-so they s-s-speak in terms of magnitude."

"But it's still like the original scale, right? Magnitude goes up in strength exponentially."

"A magnitude s-s-six releases thirty-two times more energy than a magnitude five and a thousand times more than a four."

Jack wondered how many facts and figures Wonder could keep in his head at any given time. He asked how many earthquakes occurred in California every year.

"Tens of thousands, but only two or three s-s-surpass 5.5, meaning they cause s-s-sizeable damage."

Jack finished the coffee. "We get so many because of all the fault zones here."

"We live in a s-s-subduction zone. A product of plate tectonics. There are more than two hundred known earthquake faults in the s-s-state."

"Including the big ones that run through the Bay Area. The San Andreas, the Hayward, and the... what's the third one called?"

"Rodgers Creek."

"There's a reason there's a song that says this city was built on rock and roll."

"S-S-Starship released the s-s-single on August 1, 1985. It was s-s-sung by Grace S-S-Slick. Bernie Taupin wrote the lyrics. He is best known as Elton John's longtime s-s-songwriting—"

Jack headed him off with the empty coffee mug. "Okay, okay. I believe you. But the reason I asked was because Berlin went out of his way to say he's going to look into tightening up seismic safety laws."

"It's a recent addition to his s-s-stump s-s-speech."

"The thing is, there's already plenty of laws on the books about buildings having to meet earthquake standards. Especially hospitals and old buildings. I know because when I bought the place on Mission and another building over on Guerrero Street they had to pass inspection. Berlin sounds as if he's laying the groundwork for writing a new law that would give the City the authority to condemn and redevelop."

Wonder Boy paused. "If he s-s-succeeds, that would make him very powerful if he becomes mayor."

"You know the old saying. 'Power corrupts and absolute power corrupts absolutely.' I got a pitch letter just now from Frank Penny & Son Real Estate. They're already factoring in a new seismic law into their marketing strategy. And you know what I think about coincidences."

"You always s-s-say they're only for S-S-Scientologists. Do you want me to s-s-see if Berlin's campaign is being bankrolled by the Pennys?"

"I thought you'd never ask."

Wonder pointed at Jack's mug. "Does that mean you're ready for your usual now?"

Jack smiled slyly and slipped easily into brogue. "Sure, we'll just go for one, don't you know?"

THREE MEN with Moscone Center convention passes dangling from lanyards huddled near the entrance to the Gold Rush Club. They spoke in loud but self-conscious voices as they cast nervous glances at the strip joint. The doorman looked like a defensive tackle dressed to board the team plane. Jack approached and hooked a thumb at the trio.

"Dentists or insurance salesmen?"

"Is there a difference?" he growled.

Jack slipped him a Hamilton and went inside. The lounge was dark and the stage bright. Valentine Song was wearing white boots and a matching thong with folded greenbacks tucked into the string waistband. She was pole dancing to Rhianna's "Skin" and the music was cranked up so loud the glassware behind the bar rattled. It didn't seem to bother the men at the front tables any. They didn't even bother to look down at their plates heaped with fried chicken.

A cocktail waitress dressed in a sheer teddy that didn't hide the safety pins piercing her nipples asked Jack what he wanted to drink.

"Nothing right now."

"Nothing still costs something. There's a two-drink

minimum to go along with the all-you-can-eat and all-you-can-watch. It's the best deal in town and the—"

"I know, I know." He placed a couple of bills on her tray and moved on.

He found a table in the back and caught Valentine's attention when her number was over. She joined him a few minutes later after changing into a batik sarong.

"Hi, Jack. How come you got no free food? You not hungry?"

"Maybe later. I wanted to see how you were doing. You know, after this morning and all. Make sure you were okay."

"That very sweet. You the best. Your wife one lucky woman."

"The other way around according to her. So, how are you?"

"Okay. Poor Mr. Garza. He really nice guy."

"You mind if I ask why you went to his shop this morning?"

"Oh yes, I go there plenty often. Send money to my mother. I trust him. He the best. Money always get home no problem. And he not charge too much also."

"You always go so early in the morning?"

"You talk like policeman officer. He ask same thing. I go first thing because I so busy working two jobs and going to school. If you worried, I paid you rest of money last night. You see it? I put it under door like I promised. One hundred dollar."

"I'm sure you did."

"Oh yes, you can trust me." She combed her fingers through the long fall of hair as if trying to align the purple streak.

Jack said, "Do you talk to Mr. Garza about stuff other than sending money home? Has he ever said anything about anybody? Maybe a dissatisfied customer."

"That how you say it? It not *unsatisfied*?"

"You can go either way. He ever talk about anybody?"

"Not really. I mean, we talk about money and I tell him about you, how you the best. Let me pay rent when I have it and he said he wish he had you for landlord. He say his not nice guy. Want to charge him too much or make him move."

"You know who his landlord is?"

Valentine pursed her lips. "Oh yes, but maybe better I not say."

"Why not?"

"I not want trouble at my job."

"Why would that get you into trouble?"

"Customer always right."

"So, he's the same guy at the Double Dice who's unfriendly by being too friendly."

She didn't answer but her eyes said yes.

Jack said, "I got to go, but I'll check on you later. Make sure you're okay."

"Oh yes, you the best. You sure you not want to stay and watch next number? I dress like Rati. She Hindu goddess of sex. I take clothes off to Beyonce's 'Drunk In Love.' Always get biggest tips."

## 6

The offices of Frank Penny & Son Real Estate occupied the top floor of an eight-story building on Mission Street not far from Jack's own office. When it was built in the 1970s, it was the tallest building in the neighborhood, and its pseudo modern façade reflected the forgettable architectural style of the time.

The lobby of the real estate magnate's office stood in stark contrast. It was heavy on red leather furniture and dark paneling. The walls were hung with California Real Estate Association agency-of-the-year plaques and framed photos of Penny Sr. shaking hands with dignitaries, including the San Francisco Diocese's last five archbishops. Jack cooled his heels thumbing through back issues of *Columbia*, the official magazine of the Knights of Columbus.

After waiting for thirty minutes, the receptionist ushered him to a corner office. Heavy drapes blackened the windows and the only light came from a brass desk lamp with a green shade. Penny didn't bother to get up from behind his massive oak desk. Nor did he offer to shake hands. He peered through thick glasses that made his eyes bulge.

"Your mother and I grew up on the same street." His voice was a croak. "Did you know that?"

Jack shook his head.

"We used to walk together to St. Joseph's from kindergarten through high school. Your mother never missed mass. I was saddened by her death, but she's with the Heavenly Father now." He crossed himself. "Your mother was a saint, but your father? I understand you took after him."

"Now that's a different way to start a sales pitch," Jack said.

"My receptionist told me it's you who has something to sell."

"Maybe. Your e-mail said you have an exchange buyer looking for properties. Is it for real or a come on?"

"Everything is real if you make it so. We represent many buyers. Where's your property at?"

"You know that. And you know I own more than one. You know every property in the Mission and who collects what for rent and how much they owe the bank."

"I suppose I should accept that as a compliment." Penny had rounded shoulders and no neck. He dressed as if he were going to a funeral. "Are you a serious seller or only looking for a free appraisal?"

"Maybe both."

"Nothing in life is free. Not even the Lord's forgiveness. What do you think your buildings are worth?"

"All or any one in particular?"

"Let's start with the one on Mission Street."

Jack hid his smile after Penny confirmed he knew his holdings all along. "You tell me. I never negotiate against myself."

"This isn't a negotiation. It's a conversation."

"Everything's a negotiation in real estate."

"You're new to the business, but maybe you have learned a thing or two. Here's another lesson for you: the market dictates price, not the seller."

"When it comes to the Mission, you do most of the dictating. Who's your so-called exchange buyer?"

Frank Penny Sr. cleared his throat. The sound made Jack think of a pond at night. "It doesn't matter."

"It does to me."

"In my experience, the buyer is rarely the problem. It's the seller who usually proves to be the fly in the ointment."

Now Jack pictured a frog sitting on a lily pad snatching a bug out of the air with a flick of its tongue. "How's that?"

Penny leaned back, took off his glasses, and polished the lenses with a silk cloth. Even without the glasses, his eyeballs appeared unusually large. "Sellers have unrealistic expectations of their property's worth. They let sentimentality get in the way of sound business principles. Ego, not money, is their biggest stumbling block. They take affront too easily and reject reality too readily. They fail to recognize opportunity or act in their own best interest."

"But isn't that what's happening in the Mission right now, opportunity? Real estate's booming. All these techies living four to a room got to live somewhere. Why should I sell my building? Why shouldn't I knock it down and build something even bigger?"

The property baron put back on his glasses. "Because you are an amateur. You lack the political connections to get the necessary permits. You lack a track record with architects and builders to negotiate a favorable contract. You lack banking relationships to get financing. You lack credit worthy commercial tenants with guaranteed long-term leases as collateral. You lack renters who have stable jobs. The only thing you don't lack is a lot of risk."

"I'm not averse to risk."

"I meant you are the risk. You are a risky seller."

"I don't follow."

"Your property's provenance is tainted. It's a risk for any buyer."

"My title's clear. I didn't have any problems getting ALTA insurance during escrow. I wouldn't again if I chose to sell."

Penny sighed. "Not if someone were to look more closely at the origination of your purchasing funds. Would they withstand a thorough IRS audit? How about an FBI investigation into money laundering?"

Jack returned Penny's sigh. "And here I thought you were giving me fatherly advice out of respect for my dead mama."

"But I am, I am. Your history is no secret. The last thing a typical buyer wants is to get involved in a transaction with a suspicious provenance. The deal and all the money sunk into it could get tied up by an investigation for years. It requires a very special buyer to take on your kind of risk."

"A *special buyer*? And you could find one for me, couldn't you?"

"Perhaps. But you understand the risk will impact your selling price."

"How big of an impact?"

"I would expect 50 percent on the downside."

Jack rubbed his jaw as if thinking it over. "You know something? I really don't want to sell. Don't have to. And I really don't have a problem proving how I came to buy the building. Someone wants to investigate the source of my funds, bring it on. But you know what I do have a problem with?"

"What is that?"

"Someone threatening me."

"No one is threatening you. I'm simply explaining the facts of life when it comes to real estate. As a courtesy to the memory of your mother, of course."

"And out of respect to her, I'll give you the benefit of the doubt. But I won't do the same for your son."

"What does Frank Jr. have to do with any of this?"

"Frankie and his new toy showed up at Abuelita's Restaurant and forgot to bring their table manners. *Señora* Martinez is family to me. Don't even get me started how Hark feels about somebody threatening his grandma."

"Now it sounds as if you're the one making threats."

"Not a threat. Simple fact."

Penny puffed out his cheeks and issued a croak. "Your mother would be ashamed of you talking to your elders like that."

"Actually, she'd be proud. She's the one who taught me how to stand up to bullies. She showed me every day she was married to my old man."

"We're finished here. You can show yourself out."

"Fine. I got what I wanted anyway."

"And what would that be?"

Jack stood. "Confirmation you own the building next to mine. Where Pietro Garza was gunned down."

When Frank Penny Sr. blinked, a nictitating membrane slid across his eyeballs. Jack thought of bullfrogs again and their third eyelids.

"Whatever makes you believe that?"

"Because you just told me."

~

VINNY VARGAS WAS HOLDING a clipboard when Jack pulled up to Hark's shop. The teen's face registered disappointment when he saw who was driving.

"*Chin*. I thought you might be a customer."

"You get a lot of people looking to turn a Prius into a lowrider?"

"Your whip could use some stylin'."

"Okay, how much for reupholstering the kids' car seats in tuck 'n roll?"

"You're messing with me, aren't you?"

"Hark inside?"

Vinny scowled. "He's in the back."

Jack cut through the garage. A small cubicle behind the spray booth served as a stock room. The big man was checking labels on paint cans.

"Hey, *'mano*, what's up?"

"I see your intern hasn't walked yet."

"I think of him as my apprentice."

"Same thing."

"What's that make me then?"

"His mentor."

Hark grinned. "I like the sound of that. Classy."

"I paid Frank Penny Sr. a visit. Your name came up."

"How so?"

"He made a not-so-veiled threat about calling the law on how I came to own my building. He said he'd leave the phone on the hook if I sold it to him for fifty cents on the dollar."

"I hope you threw the phone at him."

"No, but I did throw in how we both felt about Frankie making threats when he showed up at your grandma's."

"You beat me to it. I been meaning to go over there and deliver the same message myself. Let Frank Sr. know if I catch his punk ass son at my *abuelita's* again, I'll make it special delivery."

"I'd forgotten he dresses like Marlon Brando in the *Godfather*. Sitting in a room with no lights on and all sorts of religious stuff on the walls. I thought I was back at Saint Joe's with Father Bernardus warning me I was going straight to hell for chugging the communion wine."

"Old man Penny always was the church's biggest check

writer. Punching his ticket to heaven to make up for all the sins he committed cheating people out of their homes and gouging them for rent. Why did you go see him?"

"Find out if he owns the building next to mine. Where Garza was murdered."

"Can't you learn that online?"

"Commercial property deeds are usually registered to holding companies to shelter the real owner from liability. Plus, I wanted to see his face when I got him to admit it."

"Which he did, you always good at getting people to say what they don't want to say even when they don't say any words at all. What was his tell?"

"Blinks like a frog."

Hark grimaced. "Nasty. You think he had anything to do with Garza getting shot? Part of the rough stuff some landlords been giving tenants."

"I don't know for sure. The cops think it was a holdup because the safe was emptied, but Garza was already getting strong-armed for more rent. When he complained to the rent board about it, someone gave his storefront the treatment. Graffiti, glue in the lock."

"Pissant stuff to get him to pay or move out. Definitely sounds like something Frankie would do. He's always been a punk. Remember back in school? He'd go crying to the nuns you bump him in the hall. Never once took a shower after gym."

"And now he has a personal valet holding up a towel to shield his junk."

"Ricky Udo's a punk too. I asked around about him. He started off doing collections for Frank Sr. He'd show up on the day the tenants on government assistance got their checks and force them to sign them over."

"Beating up on retirees and the disabled. Cute. He must have made a name for himself to get the old man to trust him to take care of Junior."

"I heard Udo's into fight club. Participates in the private kind. A UFC wannabe. If I catch him around here, I'll deliver him a special message too."

"Hopefully it won't come to that. Frank Sr. carries a lot of weight and he's not afraid to throw it around, especially when it comes to protecting his son."

"Since when were we ever afraid of people like him?"

"Just being strategic."

"Strategic, huh? Guess that happens when you got little mouths to feed."

Hark grinned when he said it, but Jack wondered if maybe he was right.

"Let's see how it plays out. You heard Terry is heading up the murder investigation, right? Maybe he'll find Frankie and Ricky did have something to do with Garza's death and we won't have to do a thing."

"And if that doesn't pan out?"

"Then maybe we go about it in a way that hits him where it really hurts."

"You mean his wallet. Now we're talking."

## 7

J ack spent the day running the traps on his properties and was satisfied the method he'd used to source the money and create a paper trail of receipts and tax returns was foolproof. He'd always been as careful about laundering a take as he had designing the play that made the score. Walking away from a dead-bang con after sensing even the smallest of details was off had kept him out of prison. That and keeping San Francisco's top defense lawyer on retainer.

Though he was confident his real estate transactions would pass close scrutiny, his radar kept pinging. Frank Penny made the threat for a reason, and Jack's gut told him his building stood in the way of whatever the old slumlord was planning for Mission Street.

With no answers at his fingertips, he shut down his laptop and walked across the street. Little was recognizable from the old days when he opened the door to the Double Dice. It no longer reeked of stale smoke and spilled beer. The pool tables had been replaced by mid-century modern furnishings and the lighting was soft and inviting. The clientele had been updated too. A young man wearing a Guy Fawkes T-shirt was holding forth at a table crowded with fellow hipsters. He was crowing about the code he'd written for a start-up offering custom-packed suitcases.

"The user enters destination, clothing size, favorite brands, choice of toiletries, and flight information. Voilà, the selections are packed, shipped, and delivered right to their Airbnb. Swimwear, flip flops, and PABA-free sunscreen for a Hawaii vacation, designer clothes for a weekend in Paris. The suitcase comes with a return shipping label so the user never has to check luggage again."

"Did you add a menu for specialty items?" a woman with eyebrow rings asked. "Say, sex toys if you're going on a romantic getaway."

"Of course. And any electrical device that's ordered automatically comes with the country-specific plug adaptor."

Jack walked through their laughter as he made his way to a horseshoe bar in the rear. A few longtime patrons clung to it as if it were a life raft cast adrift in a frothy sea whipped by change.

"Anchor Steam," he called to the bartender.

The mixologist shook his head. "Sorry, but we do offer fifty different craft brews. May I suggest a double pale ale made with organic hops? It has a hint of pear and a long finish."

"Hold the fruit and attitude and pour me something tall and cold."

He was swallowing the first gulp when the bar's owner approached. DD Mitchell was outfitted in lumberjack chic, right down to a full beard and handlebar moustache waxed at the tips.

"If it isn't Jack McCoul. What do I owe the pleasure?"

"Long time, DD. I hardly recognize the joint. You been watching a lot of HGTV?"

DD snapped his fingers. The mixologist set up two shot

glasses and made a show of pouring from a bottle of mescal held high overhead. He didn't spill a drop.

"Actually, I'm a big fan of Charles Darwin." DD knocked back his drink. A tattoo of a pair of dice showing boxcars rode above his knuckles.

"Evolution. I hear there's a lot of that going around here these days. People adapting to changing times."

"My father taught me you don't have to be faster than a lion. You only have to be faster than the other guy running."

Jack tried the mescal. It was as smoky as a campfire. "I remember coming in here looking for my old man to tell him supper was on the table. Most of the time he and your dad were the only ones in the place. Now look at it."

"Business is good, what can I say?"

"Your dad, he opened, what, thirty, forty years ago?"

"A little longer, but yeah."

"He made a good investment. I bet back then he bought this building for next to nothing."

Jack eyed DD over his shot glass as he said it. The bar owner's change in expression told him what he wanted to know.

"I better get back to work," DD said. "Don't be a stranger."

Jack chased the mescal with the rest of his beer and then went to the men's room. When he came out he saw Valentine Song holding a tray of drinks. He could hear her voice despite the din of the crowd.

"Oh yes, please not do that. Stop please. I not want to drop my tray. Okay?"

Frank Penny Jr. was gripping her arm. "What's the matter, sweet thing, don't I get a kiss hello?"

"Oh yes, hello, Mr. Penny. I am working now. Bye-bye."

He tightened his grip. "Come on and join me for a drink."

"Oh yes, I cannot. I am working now. Thank you. Bye-bye."

"And I say have a drink with me."

Valentine seemed frozen. Her eyes swept the room. Jack was already headed her way. He said, "Hey, Frankie. How come everywhere I go you keep turning up like a bad penny?"

The real estate heir sneered. "Do you mind? I'm having a private conversation here."

"Looks a little one-sided to me."

"What's it to you?"

"I could say it's because she's my tenant so I don't want anything to interfere with her ability to pay rent, but the real reason is because you're a dick. Get your hands off her."

The junior Penny made a show of holding on, but when Jack took a step toward him, he let go. "I hear you met with my father. You'd be smart to take him up on his offer."

"What offer is that?" Jack said.

"Remember the game Monopoly? You trade him your properties for a Get Out of Jail Free card."

"Careful, Frankie. You don't want to hurt yourself trying to sound clever."

"Screw you. If this place wasn't so public, I'd—"

"What, call Ricky Udo?"

"I don't need him."

"Sure you do. He's your American Express card."

"What's that supposed to mean?"

"You never leave home without him."

The people at the nearest table laughed.

Penny reddened. "Well, he's not here right now, is he?"

Jack looked around. "Where'd he go? Oil up for fight club or fetch you a straw and umbrella for your drink?"

That earned another round of laughter. Frank Jr. turned even redder. He raised his palms as if to shove Jack in the chest, but Jack quickly grabbed them and pinned them back against the punk's chest.

"Ow!" Penny cried.

That's when DD Mitchell appeared.

"Gentlemen, how about we take this conversation outside?"

Jack said, "I was just leaving, but tell Frankie here to keep his hands in his pockets when he's around your employees. He's likely to get himself slapped."

"That'll be the day he tells me anything," Frank Jr. huffed.

DD looked as if he'd swallowed something sour, but he didn't say a word in front of his customers.

Katie wore a black sheath dress that made her emerald eyes sparkle even brighter. She and Jack were sitting at a window table at Bella Luna, a bottle of champagne chilling in a silver ice bucket beside them.

"To babysitters," Jack said as they clinked flutes. "Until someone invents an app that can change diapers, they're worth more than Elon and Zuckerberg combined."

Katie leaned forward. "Do you know this is the first date we've had in nine months?"

"Those parenting books failed to mention that part."

"But you wouldn't trade it for anything, would you?"

"I might consider swapping some of Harry's volume when he's letting us know he's hungry. Kid's got a pair of lungs on him."

"Maybe he'll be the next Irish Tenor."

"If we're lucky he'll take up a nice quiet pastime like his big sis and read books with actual words in them."

Katie sipped her champagne. "Remember, we can't compare them. Girls are different than boys."

"So you keep educating me. In and out of bed."

"Teacher's pet."

"You sure you don't want to run over and grab a room at the Fairmont? We could get a suite on the top floor with a view. Order room service."

"You're such a romantic, but I'm famished. We can go after we eat."

"Deal," he said.

On cue the waiter appeared and they ordered a Caesar to share, *gnocchi e spinaci* for her and *saltimbocca di vitello con fungo morel* for him. They ate in silence, savoring the food as much as the mood.

Katie finished the last of her gnocchi. "I'm surprised you brought me here."

"Why? It's always been our favorite. Small and local and they make the pasta by hand."

"Because it's in North Beach." She leveled her gaze on him. "Because of Grace."

Grace Millefiori was Zita's mother. She'd grown up in the shadow of Coit Tower and had been more than Jack's former lover. She'd been a partner in crime.

"Do you think of her often?" Katie asked.

"From time to time, but it's getting less and less. Death does that. The first memory to go is the sound of their voice. And then the way they moved, their mannerisms. It's the same with my mother. You always hold onto the way they looked."

"As well as their spirit," Katie added quickly. "My grandmother is like that for me. I feel her when I cook a certain dish or when I see an evening star. Not when the sky is dark, but when it still holds the last light. You can see them there, ever so pale. She'd take my hand and say, 'Stars never go away. You can always count on them.' "

"Your grandmother was wise."

Katie patted her lips with a napkin. "Do you see Grace in Zita?"

"Actually, I see more of you. You've spent more time with her than she ever did."

"That may be true, but remember the promise you made her. Zita will always know who her biological mother was."

"I haven't forgotten."

Katie ordered *tiramisu* for dessert and Jack drank a double espresso, hoping the caffeine would keep him awake all night long so he wouldn't have to relive Grace's death in his dreams again.

It was three in the morning and they were snuggling in the backseat. Katie told the driver his app was taking them the wrong way home from the Fairmont when Jack's phone buzzed. Caller ID said Pay Tel, a phone card used by inmates.

"Speak," he answered.

"Hey 'mano, call the fat man, okay? I don't got his number on me down here at the Hall."

Jack steadied his reaction so as not to reveal emotion or ask any questions. Calls from jail were never private. "You got it," he said.

Hark paused before saying, "Okay then," and hung up.

"Was that the babysitter?" Katie asked. "I told her we wouldn't be home until very late. Well, early in the morning now. Tonight was, well..." And she gave his arm a squeeze.

"It was Hark."

"What's wrong?"

"He's in jail."

"Oh my god. What happened?"

"I don't know. He didn't say and I didn't ask."

"You've got to go help him right now."

Jack tapped the driver. "Change of plans. We're going to two different places now South of the Slot."

"Where's that? Never heard of it."

Jack blew out air. Slot was the old name for Market Street when it had a cable car running up and down. He guessed the driver was from some town hours away. Many commuted all the way to the city to take advantage of more passengers and higher rates. Jack gave him the address to the Hall of Justice.

Once Katie was safely home, he texted Cicero Broadshank with a 911. The lawyer returned the call immediately.

"Jack, my boy. Given the hour I can only assume the worst. What is it?"

"Hark's been arrested. I need you to call the Hall and see what's up. I'm on my way there now."

The portly lawyer yawned. "Certainly to the former, but I must strongly advise against the latter. Arrest, no matter how minor the infraction, is nothing to be trifled with. Best to leave interfacing with the authorities to members of the bar."

"No worries. I won't raise a ruckus or say a word, but I need to suss things out and line up bail. Hark's not one to sit quietly. And there could be others in there who won't let him. You know his past."

"Listen to me carefully. You must exercise all due caution until we ascertain the exactitude of the situation. Furthermore, I require your verbal assent that your retainer applies to Mr. Martinez effective immediately."

"It does. You don't even have to ask."

"But I do, my boy. It is for Mr. Martinez's protection as well as my own. This way we have established attorney-client privilege which provides me with the latitude I require to operate on his behalf."

"I assent."

"Then I will place the necessary calls forthwith, but it may be to no avail given it is not even dawn."

The driver stopped in front of an imposing granite building at 850 Brannan Street that housed courtrooms, three floors of cells, and San Francisco Police Department's Operational Headquarters, better known as Southern Station.

"Could you give me a five-star rating before you get out?" the driver asked. "You know, in case you get tossed in the jug. I hear they take your phone away."

Jack started to say something, but then breathed in, breathed out. It was a relaxation technique Katie had taught him. Sometimes it even worked. He exited without saying a word, much less punching in a review.

Despite the hour a line snaked from the front door as people waited to pass through the metal detectors. Bus stop lawyers and bail bond agents trolled for clients. Homeless people huddled under grimy blankets at both ends of the building. Jack held his breath as he prepared to step into the maw of a criminal justice system that would put him behind bars too if it could.

S ecurity turned out to be a breeze—Jack never carried, believing if he needed a gun he'd screwed up the play from the get-go—but tiptoeing through the San Francisco Zoo's infamous tiger den would be easier than bullshitting his way past Southern Station's night shift gatekeeper. Her name was Sergeant Dawn Bottho, better known as Don't Bother. From thirty feet away she looked scary. From ten feet away she looked like thirty feet was a wise place to retreat to. Her vocabulary was restricted to variations of *no*, *beat it*, and *do-you-want-me-to-hurt-you.*

Jack bellied up to the transom and took the saccharine approach as he leaned toward the voice speak thru in the bullet-proof window. "Top of the evening, Sergeant Bottho. It's a pleasure to see you again, don't you know?"

"Can the brogue, McCoul. The only way you're getting inside is if you're wearing cuffs or riding a stretcher. Take your pick."

"What a generous offer, but I'm here on official business."

"And what business would that be? Conning uniformeds out of their pensions by selling timeshares on the moon?"

Jack faked a laugh and doubled down on flattery. "Have you considered doing stand-up at Cobbs?"

"Don't make me get out of this chair."

"Seriously, I'm here as a representative for Broadshank, Hicklin, and Wong. The firm has received information that a client may be in detention. I was dispatched to verify."

"Cut the crap. You don't work for Broadass."

The amply proportioned desk sergeant shifted in her roller chair. It's groan of protest was as loud as Jack's as he switched tactics.

"Come on, Sarge. Do us both a favor and let me in so I can find out what's what. It'll spare you a visit from CB himself. Don't you want a nice, quiet shift?"

"I don't do nice."

"Okay, have it your way. By the way, when Lieutenant Dolan asks, would you let him know I tried to talk to him?"

"And why would Dolan stop what he's doing to talk to you?"

Jack filed the information. So, Terry was there.

"The Garza murder. You know, two birds, one stone. I was going to give him some new information while I was here checking on the welfare of our client. I sent Dolan a text letting him know I'd stop by."

"You don't even know how to tell the truth, do you?"

"A Benjamin says I am. Go ahead, call him and see."

"Are you trying to bribe me?"

"It's not a bribe, it's a bet."

"I could run you in for gambling."

"If I'm right, you don't have to pay me a thing. If I'm wrong, I'll make a donation to the donuts kitty. Is it still that old Folger's can with the slit in the plastic lid?"

Her glare didn't waver, but finally she reached under the counter and hit the buzzer. The security door to the squad room unlatched.

"If you even try to say *thank you*, they'll be your last words," she snarled.

Jack gave her a wink and hurried through the door. The floor was quiet because of the hour. He ran into no interference as he headed straight toward the back where Dolan had a cubicle. The homicide detective wasn't at his desk so Jack climbed aboard the visitor's chair and pulled out his phone.

"What did you find out?" he said when Cicero Broadshank picked up. "Is it a DUI or a disturbing the peace? Don't tell me he got in a fight and broke some guy's arm."

"Where are you?"

"I'm here at the Hall."

"I mean your exact location as of present. That granite fortress is a labyrinth."

"Terry Dolan's office."

"My god, boy," Broadshank bellowed. "Do not tell me he is holding you as an accessory. Say nothing to incriminate yourself."

"Accessory to what?"

"I will tell you after I speak with someone with authority at the district attorney's office. It has been a trial raising anyone other than a first-year law student at this ungodly hour. Do not say a word to Lieutenant Dolan."

"I won't if you tell me why Hark is here."

Broadshank sighed. "Mr. Martinez is being held as a suspect in a homicide."

"Whose?"

But the connection broke before he responded.

JACK HAD A LONG WAIT. He spent the time guessing who the victim was and what connection they had to Hark. Faces flashed as Jack ran through past run-ins and grievances. The list of names was not short.

Terry Dolan's arrival brought his speculation to a halt. "What are you doing here?" the cop asked.

"Hark made his one call."

"He wasted it on you."

"So, you were upstairs with him. Okay, glad we got that out of the way. Whatever you're trying to pin on him, he didn't do it."

The detective showed a mix of exhaustion and irritation. "What do you know?"

"I know Hark, and that's good enough for me."

"So do I. Remember, we all went to the same school. One of us even studied."

"I called Cicero Broadshank. He'll be in the house any second if he isn't already. You know how he loves to file police brutality suits."

Terry slapped a manila folder on the desk. It was thin, but Jack knew it would fatten with time. It was a murder book. He searched for the victim's name on the index tab, but it was purposely placed face down.

"You're wasting your time if you think I'm going to help you," Terry said.

"I'm not asking for it. CB will have him walking out the door in time for breakfast."

"Don't count on it."

"And don't you count on Hark being guilty of anything."

Terry shuffled some papers around. "The only reason you're still sitting here is because Sergeant Bottho called me and said you had information about the Garza murder. It's your lucky day if you told her the truth. If not, she's going to come in here and arrest you for attempting to bribe an officer."

Jack didn't miss a beat. "I got something, all right. Garza was having problems with his landlord. He filed a complaint after they jacked up his rent and tried to force him out. That earned him a storefront covered in graffiti. He filed another complaint. That could be your probable cause. Maybe they came back to shut him up for good."

"All renters think they're being overcharged. I'm a renter and I think so too."

"Does your landlord beat you up if you complain?"

"You're wasting my time. Get out of here."

"I own the building next door to Garza's shop. I know a thing or two about tenant landlord relations. Things are getting tense in the Mission."

"Real estate is quite a change of pace for you."

"Yeah, I'm all settled down. Wife, two kids, and a mortgage." He let it sit before jabbing it home. "Katie, she always wants to be making babies."

Terry's jaw tightened. "How long have you owned the building?"

Jack told him.

"How long has Miss Song been your tenant?"

"I'd have to look at my records, but she was living there when I bought the place. Why?"

"The man who runs the shoe store, Sami Alfassi, was he already a tenant too?"

Terry had taken night classes at Golden Gate Law and Jack figured he'd learned enough to know the answer before he ever asked a question.

"The space was empty when I bought it. I leased it to him. Why?"

The detective's rep tie hung so straight it was as if weights were attached to the tips. "Did you conduct a background check before letting him move in?"

"Are you saying that because he's Syrian?"

"I'm saying it because I'm investigating a murder."

"I'm in the rental business, not Homeland Security. I like Alfassi, I liked his business plan. Plus, he paid the first month and security up front."

"We'll see about that."

"Knock yourself out. And while you're at it, knock on the hundred other businesses and over-the-store apartments on the street. You'll get the same answer."

"And what's that?"

"Some landlords are hassling tenants big time. If I were you, I'd look into Garza's."

Terry shuffled some papers. "That's your hot tip? I should investigate the building owner because he raised Garza's rent?"

"There's a bigger picture if you care to look."

"And what would that be?"

"You grew up in the Mission. You see how fast it's changing. A lot of money is pouring in and longtime tenants like Garza are getting squeezed out. Old buildings are getting bought up and knocked down."

"It's called redevelopment. It happens all over the city."

"Yeah, but this time it's different. I think Garza was killed to send a message."

"We're done here."

Jack said, "Remember when we were kids? The space I rented to Alfassi used to be a toy store. Pop Harrigan's. Sold LEGO, baseball equipment, games, you name it. Pop would line the new bikes in a row out on the street and didn't bother to lock them up. He'd let you borrow one to ride up and down the street."

"No, he didn't. You stole them."

"Whatever I borrowed from Pop Harrigan I always returned. It was the way the neighborhood used be."

"You're lucky my father didn't catch you in the act. He would've busted you."

"Speaking of beat cops, it sure sounds like they'll be making a comeback if Supervisor Berlin has his way. Who knows, maybe you can step into your dad's blacks after Berlin strips you of your gold bar."

"And why would he do that?"

"Because he needs a fall guy to show he's serious about law and order while he's campaigning. He can't afford to take on the chief so he'll go after someone lower on the food chain. Someone who has a shiny reputation he can tarnish. The shinier the better because reporters like Shauna Rhames are no different than crows; they can't resist picking up bright objects."

"You'll say anything to try and get me to tell you why Hark is upstairs."

"Maybe. But maybe I'm also on to something about Berlin. Remember when we were playing ball back at Saint Joe's? Junior year, there was a kid transferred over from the East Bay. A big left-hander from Bishop O'Dowd. Lonnie Jones."

"What does Lonnie Jones have to do with anything?"

"The only way for Lonnie to get college scouts to notice him was to knock off the team's number one starter."

"But he never did. I held the position all through varsity."

"But Lonnie tried and Lonnie failed. You can thank Hark for that."

Terry smacked the top of his desk. "I kept my starting spot because of my ERA. I have two MVP awards and a college scholarship to prove it."

"Don't forget Hark caught every game you threw. He won the Father Bernardus Award for Best Team Player. Hark took Lonnie out for a drive after practice one day. Told him how throwing an inning or two of relief was a helluva lot better than a busted throwing arm."

Terry smacked the desk again. "I'm not going to tell you anything about Hark's arrest."

"I don't need you to. Broadshank will. But what I said about Garza's beef with his landlord is solid. And it's the tip of the iceberg. Dig around and you'll find other shopkeepers are getting hassled too."

"They should take it to a tenants' rights group. There's a bunch in town. Now, I have a murder case to work."

"I'm telling you, look into Garza's being strong-armed by his landlord."

"Okay, if it'll get you out of here, give me the name."

"Frank Penny & Son Real Estate."

The cop threw a protective hand over the manila folder. When he did, Jack's stomach dropped.

## 10

C icero Broadshank and Jack stood in a cramped room reserved for lawyers that was on the same floor as the holding cells. The way the portly lawyer explained it, Frank Penny Jr.'s body was discovered in Osage Alley, a narrow backstreet that ran parallel to Mission Street. Preliminary cause was blunt force trauma.

A woman whose second-floor bedroom overlooked the alleyway was awakened by loud voices. She looked out the window and saw a man crumpled on the pavement as another man hurried away. An officer in a passing patrol car fielded the 911 dispatcher's call and spotted the suspect. He gave chase down Osage. A second patrol car set up an intercept at Twenty-Fourth Street, but the suspect managed to evade the waiting officer and cut over to Bartlett, another narrow street that ran parallel. The first patrol car kept chase while the second raced to Valencia, turned right, and turned right again on Twenty-Second. The suspect ducked into a parking lot alongside Hark's garage. The cops radioed for backup and then stormed the shop.

Hark was in the bathroom bandaging his knuckles when they burst in with guns drawn. He explained he'd been working late and injured himself pounding the dents out of an '87 Regal's fender. They weren't in a listening mood. They slammed him to the floor, slapped the cuffs on, and raced him to the Hall with sirens blaring. While a robbery homicide team took turns questioning him, the patrol officers returned to the neighborhood. A canvas turned up a witness who said he'd overheard Hark and Frank Penny Jr. arguing outside the Double Dice.

"And all this took place over the span of a couple of hours?" Jack asked.

"It is surprising that the police moved with such alacrity," Broadshank replied. "Not only is the speed in which they charged him unusual, but so is the fact they declined to exercise a forty-eight hours' hold in order to give investigators additional time to gather evidence. Rarely do they relinquish that so readily."

"Have you spoken to him?"

"Only cursorily. By the time I arrived, Mr. Martinez had already been processed. We met in a room reserved for attorneys and their clients. While there are assurances it is not monitored, I always limit the conversation to avoid inadvertent admissions or incriminations."

"What did he tell you?"

"It was I who did the majority of the talking. I conveyed to him I was his legal representative and advised him to say nothing to the investigators or anyone who might purport to be another inmate."

"It's not Hark's first rodeo. He won't give up anything more than name, rank, and serial number."

"Ah, yes, now I recall. He served in the armed forces. The recipient of a Purple Heart or two, if I remember correctly. That speaks highly of his character and should help."

"You say the cops broke into his shop and found him in the john. They have a warrant?"

"No, but since they were in the pursuit of a suspected murderer, they did not need one. Probable cause and public safety supersede the necessity of a court order or judge's verbal assent."

"Hark told them he'd been there all night working, right?"

Broadshank nodded.

"So, what about somebody who can vouch for him? An alibi? Hark's got a kid living there, an employee. Works on the cars during the day and crashes on the office couch while he's doing duty as night watchman. His name's Vinny Vargas. What did Vinny say?"

"Strange, Mr. Martinez did not mention another party present at the locale. Nor did the police report anybody. At least not to my knowledge based on a perfunctory interview I conducted with the booking officer."

Jack rubbed his jaw. "That doesn't add up. Vinny's taken to the shop like a barnacle. Couldn't scrape him off if you tried. I'll run down what's up with that."

Broadshank checked his watch. "I am afraid our time in this rather malodorous facility is limited. We will have an opportunity to discuss the matter further."

"Any chance I can see him?"

"Not tonight, my boy. He has already been transferred to a cell on the seventh floor. You will have to wait until his arraignment."

Jack sucked his teeth. "Arraignment's only a formal reading of the charges and making a plea."

"Precisely. There should be no surprises as a homicide charge typically begins at murder in the first degree to provide the prosecutor room within which to negotiate. My clients always plead innocent, of course."

Broadshank straightened the lapels of his jacket. He wore a coal black suit with white chalk stripes and a yellow silk tie and matching pocket hanky. His courtroom baritone, expensive clothes, and mane of white hair were carefully cultivated to impress jurors and intimidate the low paid staff attorneys with the district attorney's office.

Jack asked about bail.

"Bail for murder one is rare, but I am cautiously optimistic it may be proffered. We should be prepared that it is likely to be an obscene amount. Seven figures would not surprise me. Naturally, I will make the case for a lower amount. Release on his own recognizance is out of the question at present."

Jack considered how much cash he could put his hands on. He'd need to come up with $100,000 minimum for the up-front fee plus sign over the deed to his building on Mission Street as collateral.

"We need to get him out of jail fast," Jack said. "Hark's got history when he was a young banger. There could be someone in lockup right now looking to make a name for himself."

"I will do my best to expedite release, but, alas, there appears to be extenuating circumstances. The district attorney's office indicated I should expect little quarter, and Mr. Martinez even less."

"How come?"

"The victim's father is Frank Penny Sr. He is a man of considerable influence and will indubitably remind his friends on the police commission of that. I am sure he will deploy every means at his disposal to avenge his son's death."

Jack sucked his teeth again. "I expect there's going to be lots of media attention."

"That, my boy, is a certitude. I presume members of the fourth estate are already congregating on the steps of this very building."

"Are you going down to proclaim Hark's innocence?"

"Certainly not. There would be no advantage at this point. I shall wait until after the arraignment and, depending on its outcome, assess the advantages and disadvantages of trying the case in the court of public opinion." He took a breath. "You can be sure the district attorney will be weighing the merits of press coverage as well. It is campaign season, after all, and she is running for reelection."

That made Jack think of Supervisor Erick Berlin. Wonder Boy said he and Shauna Rhames were lovers. It was a good bet the power couple were sitting up in bed right now plotting a televised exclusive for the morning news show.

"Just so you know," Jack said. "Not for a second do I think Hark killed Frankie."

"What you and I believe has absolutely no bearing on the outcome," Broadshank said. "The only items of consequence are the body of evidence and the fortitude of the district attorney to prosecute the case to the fullest extent of the law."

## 11

B y 8:00 a.m. two other TV news vans had joined the Action News van parked out front of the Hall of Justice. Intense media coverage wasn't the only thing Cicero Broadshank had predicted correctly. So was the DA's warning about no quarter. The court had prioritized Hark's arraignment, making it number one on the docket. Jack had barely enough time to find a seat before the clerk said, "All rise!"

The judge entered through a door behind the bench and took his seat.

"Court is now in session, Judge Horatio Chun, presiding."

The clerk stated a case number. Cicero Broadshank neared the bench and remained standing. A door opened and two look-alike sheriffs ushered in Hark. He was wearing an orange jump-suit and his wrists were handcuffed and attached by a chain to a waist strap. He shuffled on rubber shower sandals, his legs manacled at the ankles. Jack tried to get eye contact with him, but it was as if Hark was staring at a wall.

The clerk stated the case number again and recited the criminal charges that had been filed against one Geraldo Santiago Martinez. They included murder in the first degree, aggravated assault, battery, possession of a firearm, resisting arrest, destruction of public property, and threatening an official.

"Why not add walking a dog without a leash?" Jack muttered.

The man sitting next to him leaned over. "Word to the wise, bro. Don' let the judge catch you talkin'. That be the Right Honorable Cowboy Chun up there. I got it on good authority he packs a pearl handle Colt .45 six-shooter under that robe. He sent mo' people to Quentin than any."

The judge asked the clerk if the defendant had been given a written copy of the complaint.

"He has, your Honor."

"And does he have legal representation present?"

"I am his attorney-in-fact." Cicero Broadshank's voice resonated like a bassoon. "May it please the court—"

Judge Chun cut him off with a wave of the gavel. "It may not. You know this is only an arraignment, Counselor. Do not waste the court's time."

The judge turned to Hark. "How do you plead?"

Hark's expression remained blank. "Not guilty."

"So noted. You are hereby bound over. A preliminary hearing is set for ten court days from today." He banged his gavel. "Next."

"But your Honor," Broadshank bellowed. "You have not addressed the issue of bail. My client is entitled—"

"Denied. Next."

Broadshank added outrage to his tenor. "But Mr. Martinez is a decorated member of the United States military, a small business owner, a respectable member of San Francisco's Latino community, and—"

"You're pushing contempt, Counselor. You may get away with that sort of behavior at a juried trial, but not in arraignment.

Bound over. Bail denied. Next case." He pounded his gavel again.

The uniformed Bobbsey Twins turned Hark around and shoved him through the door. Jack knew it opened onto a narrow hallway that led to an elevator. Hark would be whisked back to a cell on the seventh floor. It would be a nonstop ride unless the two sheriff's deputies opted to stop the car between floors and mete out a lesson in jailhouse etiquette.

Jack cornered Broadshank outside the courtroom. "Can't you appeal the bail decision?"

"Alas, I fear not. It is most unfortunate that Mr. Martinez drew Judge Chun today, an assignment I am disinclined to accept as arbitrary, given the heightened attention the crime has commanded."

"You mean the fix was in."

"It is nothing anyone could prove, mind you, but clearly the rush to arrest and arraign appears to have coincided in the prosecutor's favor with the rotating schedule of justices."

"At least if it goes to the next step, Hark can't draw Chun again."

"On the contrary, my dear boy. There is nothing to prevent that very thing from occurring as there is no perceivable or provable conflict of interest on the part of the judge. Not only can Judge Chun preside over the preliminary hearing, but he could also serve as judge on a juried trial. The only judicial step he is precluded from is if a verdict were to be appealed."

"Talk about rolling snake eyes three times in a row. We've got to stop it from going that far."

"That is my intent, and an endeavor I shall pursue with all due haste. To that end, I must return to my office immediately."

"Heads up. The media are in a feeding frenzy downstairs."

"I am well aware. Fortunately, I am entitled to the use of an alternative egress that is more private in nature."

"Backdoor man, eh?"

"A word of advice," Broadshank said. "Please do Mr. Martinez the courtesy of declining any interaction with members of the press and law enforcement. It will come to no good, I assure you."

Jack took the stairs to the first floor. There was little room to sidestep the commotion outside the front door. A quiver of microphones sprouted from the front of a portable podium that had been positioned on the top stair. A scrum of print, online, radio, and TV reporters were jockeying a few steps below as Supervisor Berlin spoke.

The man who'd cautioned Jack in the courtroom was observing from the sidelines. Jack asked what he'd missed.

"I figured the dude was your homey. You think Cowboy Chun gave him the shaft, the man up there is really stickin' it to him. What he do, cap the Supervisor's BFF and run off with his baby mama?"

"Wrong place at the wrong time is all."

"You mean wrong color at the wrong place. Ain't we all. Seems the man up there got that message. He's been saying the Mission's a shitstorm on account of your homey, who he's blamin' for everythin' from spittin' on the sidewalk to gunnin' down store owners. Say law-abidin' folks got a right to havin' somebody run this city who keep 'em safe, namely his truly."

Jack turned his attention to the podium. Berlin pivoted from outrage over Frank Penny Jr.'s death to touting the need for a seismic safety law as the solution to the city's ills. "Not only can we clean up crime in the Mission, but we can solve the housing crisis too. It's a win-win for everyone."

He flashed a campaign poster smile as the TV cameras zoomed and still cameras clicked. Someone started clapping. The crowd joined in like Pavlov's dogs. Jack looked to see who'd initiated the applause. It was Shauna Rhames.

## 12

The main streets that bisected the heart of the Mission District—Valencia, Guerrero, Dolores—were testaments to the district's cultural heritage, but it was the narrow backstreets that held its secrets.

Jack stood at the spot along Osage Alley where the younger Penny's blood still stained the sidewalk. A bordering chain link fence with wooden slats was a gallery of graffiti. Brightly sprayed hollows, fills, and end to ends covered them along with the back walls of commercial buildings whose front doors opened onto Mission Street. If the writing held any clues, Jack couldn't decipher them. He recognized a few all city artists' tags so he snapped pictures of the signatures. Maybe they'd know something.

He looked up at the second floor of the apartment building bordering the west side of the street. A bathroom window was frosted. Another darkened with blackout shades. Maybe a day sleeper's bedroom, he guessed. A third window had lacy curtains. He felt a pair of eyeballs tracking his every movement from the other side of the lace. They probably belonged to the woman who'd dialed 911.

Osage was only two and a half blocks long. Jack walked toward its terminus at Twenty-Fourth Street. Before he reached it, a delivery truck turned in and stopped. The driver got out and walked around to the back and opened the roll-up door.

Jack eased past the truck. "No one cares if you're blocking the way?"

The driver was loading a dolly. When he hoisted a case of beer, a King Kong head tattooed on his bicep bared its teeth. "You need to get a car out, give me a sec."

"No worries," Jack said. "Who's your customer, the Double Dice?"

The guy looked up. "You with the City or something?"

"I was going to get the door for you."

"Sure you were."

"I was on my way to talk to DD, but if you want to do it, suit yourself."

The beer man loaded the case and reached for another. "Sorry. You get all types in this alley. I use it because it beats double-parking on Mission. I don't mind the punks trying to grab a box of brew when I go inside, but the yuppies leaving notes on my windshield whining about not being able to get their fancy scooters past? Screw 'em."

"Millennials. That's who they are. Yuppies grew old and moved to the burbs."

"Ain't that the truth."

"Come on, I'll hold the door."

Jack walked over to a cement stoop. The bar's back door was made of steel. It was covered in graffiti too. He gave it a couple of raps. He glanced around as he waited for someone to answer. A can was filled with cigarette butts. A cardboard box held a few empties.

The door swung open. DD's eyes narrowed. "What are you doing here?"

"Just getting the door for your beer delivery."

DD looked past him. His lumberjack beard bobbed. He pushed the door wide, kicked a rubber stopper to hold it open, and joined Jack on the back stoop.

"And you were passing by, thought you'd be neighborly?"

Jack said, "I was checking out where Frankie Penny died."

"That's some bad business. I heard about it."

"When it happened or on the news?"

"When the cops knocked on my door and started asking questions." His tone turned. "What is this, anyway?"

"Friends looking out for friends. They're trying to pin it on Hark."

Jack kept his gaze fixed on DD. The bar owner shrugged.

"You know him, right?" Jack said.

"A dude with his rep, who doesn't? But do you mean, do I *know* him? Does he drink in my establishment, watch the game with me? I've seen him around. That's it."

"But Frankie Jr.'s a different story. He didn't seem like he was a stranger when I was here the other night." He let it hang.

DD didn't rush to fill the void. After a minute or so, he said, "Penny's been coming around a lot lately. He's a customer, nothing more."

"But the customer is always right."

The bartender didn't pick it up.

Jack waited and then said, "His old man owns the building, doesn't he?"

DD shrugged. "So?"

"I'm guessing Frankie thought it was something he could hold over you. Make it so you had to turn a blind eye when he acted like an asshole to your cocktail waitress."

"I don't turn a blind eye to anything. Penny wants to jack up my rent, he's going to have to wait a long time. I got twenty years left on my lease. He gets a little bump every five years, but that's as far as it goes."

Jack was about to say unless there was a fire or an earthquake, but the words suddenly stuck in his throat. "Was Frankie the only one hassling Valentine or are there others?"

"It's a bar. She's good looking and friendly. You do the math."

"I mean, anyone on the same level of assholedry as Frankie?"

DD squinted. "Are you asking me if he and some other dude got in a fight over her?"

"Wouldn't be the first time punches got thrown over a woman."

"If that's the case, I wouldn't know. If someone else has their target set on Valentine, I wouldn't know either. Most of my customers are more in love with their phones than flesh and blood. Even when they're having drinks with each other, they spend most of the time doing Snapchat, Instagram, taking selfies."

"The cops say a witness heard Hark threaten Frankie outside your place."

"They asked me about that too and I told them what I just told you. I didn't see or hear anything."

"But you know who dropped the dime on Hark."

"I may have given the Double Dice a facelift, but everyone knows the rule stayed the same as Vegas."

"*What happens here, stays here.*"

"You got that straight."

"But this so-called witness said he heard it outside. So, there you go. Your rule doesn't apply beyond the front door. Come on, DD. Who was it?"

The delivery guy made another run past with the dolly. On his way back out, he said, "See ya next time."

DD said, "Don't forget our standing order for Pliny the Elder. As much as you can get, we'll take."

"You and everybody else."

As the truck started backing up, Jack said, "How about it. Who was it?"

DD looked down at the tat on his hand rolling boxcars. "I heard it was Ricky Udo, but don't quote me on it."

## 13

S ami Alfassi wasn't standing outside the front door of his shop as usual. The yellow crime tape was also gone from the front of Garza's shop. Jack hesitated before taking the stairs up to his office. Something didn't feel right so he opened the door to the shoe store. No customers were inside. There was no sign of Alfassi either.

Jack sucked his teeth and walked toward the rear where a partition separated the store from the rear storeroom. Plaintive murmurs coming from the other side made him halt. He reached for something he could use as a weapon. The closest object was a pair of women's black stilettos. He grabbed one and held it spiked heel out and approached the opening.

Sami Alfassi was on his knees with his forehead touching a small rug, his hands palms down by his ears. He lifted his head, turned his hands palm up, murmured some more, and then lowered his forehead to the rug. Jack backed up as quickly and quietly as he could. He placed the shoe back on a rack.

When Alfassi came out, Jack said, "Sorry. Didn't mean to disturb you."

"You did not nor could not. *Dua* is a bond between Allah and man. It is not possible to disrupt it."

"I didn't see you out front, so I wondered where you were."

"My faith requires prayer multiple times a day. You are not an observant man?"

"I was raised Catholic but don't believe you need a preacher and pews to believe what you want to believe in."

"A place of worship is what you make it. I have asked for Allah's help in a mosque, in a building being shelled, and while being chased across a desert."

"Well, glad to see everything is okay. What with Garza being gunned down and now the murder around the corner, it made me wonder where you were." Jack started to turn toward the door.

"Thank you for your concern," Alfassi said. "You will join me for tea now."

"I'd be honored."

The shoe store owner disappeared into the back room. When he returned he carried two stools that he placed one on either side of the counter that held a cash register.

"Sit," he said.

They both did. Jack wondered who was going to bring the tea. He didn't have to wonder long. A teenage girl carried in a tray. She wore a hijab and jeans. Her only makeup was dark eyeliner. She set the tray down between them. It held a porcelain teapot and two cups on saucers.

"My daughter," Alfassi said. "Rima, this is Mr. McCoul. He is our landlord."

She dipped her chin but did not speak.

Jack said, "Pleased to meet you."

The girl returned to the back room.

"Is she your only child?" Jack asked.

Alfassi poured the tea. He added three spoonfuls of sugar to his and stirred. "I also have a son. Farid. He is twelve. Rima is fourteen."

"Do they go to school here in the Mission?"

"Rima does." The shopkeeper sipped the tea. "She helps me with the store at times. Farid requires more assistance with his learning so he attends a special school."

Jack tried the tea. It was strong.

Alfassi continued speaking in his matter-of-fact way. "A rocket struck Farid's classroom when he was eight years old. An accident, the government man called it. Collateral damage, I believe, is the term the American military uses. Farid has never fully recovered from seeing his classmates and instructors incinerated. The journey from Syria was very difficult for him too. He watched his mother die."

Jack tightened his grip on the tea cup. "Condolences for your loss. I can't imagine what you've been through."

"Destiny is not ours to question."

"This special school your son attends, is it nearby?"

"It is not as close as I would wish. Since I lack a car, it requires taking the autobus. Sometimes I accompany him and sometimes Rima does. Oftentimes another parent is able to drive him home. She is most generous."

They continued drinking their tea. Alfassi said, "I understand the authorities have arrested the man they say is responsible for murdering the son of the wealthy landowner."

"Yes, but he didn't do it," Jack said.

"You sound very sure of that."

"I am. I know him."

Alfassi made a face. "I too have had acquaintances arrested by the government for crimes they did not commit."

Jack glanced at Alfassi's crooked finger, the scar that ran through his eyebrow. "And you, were you also arrested?"

The shoe store owner placed his cup back in its saucer.

"Everyone who lives in Syria is under arrest, whether they are placed in a cell or left to live among the ruins."

"But you got out."

"It was Allah's will." He shook a cigarette out of a pack, and held it between his fingers, but did not light it. "And do you find it strange that the police were so quick to arrest your friend while Mr. Garza's murder remains unsolved?"

"Different situations," Jack said.

"Perhaps. But it is not so different in my country. One victim is a poor shopkeeper working hard to put food on the table and shoes on his children's feet. The other is the son of a rich and powerful man. No matter the country, the police always work harder when the men who control the purse are affected."

"What have you heard about the Garza investigation?"

"That is the problem. Not much of anything. Your friend from Robbery and Homicide has made a few appearances in the neighborhood and questioned a few of the shopkeepers, including myself, yet no arrests have been made."

"As far as these kinds of things go, it hasn't been that long."

"Perhaps the police will charge your friend with the murder of Mr. Garza in addition to the rich man's son."

"They'd have to make a case first."

"The government man running for mayor would like that. This Supervisor Berlin."

"You follow local politics?"

"Certainly. All politics are local. The same is true in Syria no matter which foreign countries help the regime or the revolution. Remember the story I told you about my home and how I owned one brick and the president nine?"

"I do," Jack said.

"I would think some might find the Supervisor's call for a new earthquake safety law is not all that different."

"You're very perceptive for someone who claims he wishes only to sell shoes," Jack said.

Alfassi bowed slightly. His hooded eyes gave nothing away.

JACK KNOCKED on Valentine Song's door before unlocking his office.

"Oh yes, who is there, please?"

"It's Jack. I wanted to see how you're holding up."

The door opened a crack. "Oh yes, hello, thank you very much. You are the best. I am fine, thank you."

"You working today?"

"Oh yes, I am going to Gold Rush. I oversleep this morning. But everything fine. Thank you very much."

"You hear about Frank Penny Jr.?"

The door opened a little wider. "Oh yes, it terrible. He not always polite, but it not nice to say now that he is dead."

"Were you working at the Double Dice that night?"

She combed the long fall of hair with her fingers. "Only a little while. I left work before closing. I have big exam for my computer class at City College and need to study. DD say it okay."

"Have the police questioned you about Frankie?"

She draped her hair over her breast and aligned the purple streak. "Why? I not know anything. I not there when he died like when I went to Mr. Garza's and he already dead and I call police. How could I call about Mr. Penny if I not there?"

"I thought they might have called you. You know, because Frankie had been hassling you. Lots of people saw him doing it. DD too. It sounds like nobody told the cops about it or they would've questioned you."

"Maybe DD did tell them. Maybe he say I was not there so they not need to ask me anything. Okay?"

"Sure, I wanted to make sure you were all right."

"I am fine. Thank you very much. Bye-bye, Jack. You the best."

As she started to push the door closed, Jack said, "The night I told Frankie to quit bothering you, did he and DD say anything to each other after I left?"

"I not sure what you mean."

"DD told Frankie and me to take it outside. We didn't because I walked away. But I got the feeling that wasn't the end of it between them."

"I have tray of drinks to give to customers. I not hear anything."

"But if Frankie had gotten out of line with you, DD would've stopped him. He being your boss and all."

"Oh yes, DD a very good boss. He pay me every week. He not take tips like some bosses. He let me come late and leave early like when I have big exam at City College."

"You like DD."

"Oh yes, I like him. He the best."

"And he likes you."

"He very nice to me."

"Nice because he's your boss or nice because he wants to be your boyfriend?"

Valentine combed her hair with her fingers again. "You the best, Jack, but I go now and get ready for dancing at Gold Rush. I see you later. Okay?"

## 14

Zita was reading on the couch. A leaning tower of books teetered on the coffee table. Harry lay on a blanket and gurgled at the ceiling. Katie was whirring something green in the blender as two pots and a pan simmered on the stove. The scene of domesticity struck Jack how different their life was from Sami Alfassi's and Valentine Song's by virtue of birthplace.

"Oh, home on the range," he called out, swept up Katie, and gave her a twirl around the kitchen. Zita giggled. Harry gurgled some more. Katie let out a shriek and told him to put her down because her kale and yogurt salad dressing was getting over whipped.

"Blenders don't come with safe words now?" he said.

She punched his shoulder and feigned shock. "Jack, the children."

He tossed his jacket on a chair and went to the fridge. With a quick twist of a corkscrew he opened a bottle of Pinot Grigio and poured two glasses.

"Mmm," Katie said as she sampled hers. "Why are you in such a good mood?"

"Just appreciating what I got."

"Does this mean they freed Hark?"

The feeling of contentment left as quickly as it had come. "Not yet." He gave a rundown of the day.

"Isn't there anything Cicero can do?"

"He's working it. So am I. But we need time to pull something together."

Katie waved her glass of wine. "Have you spoken to Hark yet?"

"Tomorrow. He's scheduled for a meeting with CB to discuss the upcoming prelim. I'll tag along as a member of the legal team."

"Tell him I'm worried about him."

"No can do, babe. Hark can't be thinking about what his people on the outside are going through. The cops and cellies will pick up on it and use it against him. He's got to focus on what's in front of him, namely putting out the vibe that nobody better fu—" Jack caught himself. "Mess with him."

He glanced over at the couch. Zita's eyes were on a book. Jack raised his chin in her direction and said to Katie, "Better we pick this up after bedtime."

"Zita, come help me with dinner, please," Katie said. "It's almost ready."

Jack watched the sky turn mauve. A flock of seagulls flew by. He picked up Harry and plopped him in a high chair. Katie and Zita carried in serving dishes. They ate family style.

Zita said, "I want to go to school."

"But you're already in school," Katie said.

"Preschool is for babies. I want to go to real school."

"And you will next fall," Katie said.

She pouted. "*Estoy listo ahora.*"

Katie shot Jack a help-me-out-here look.

Jack said, "You may be ready now, *mija*, but the advantage of the preschool you're going to is it's not every day, all day. That gives you time to go to *Abuelita's* and teach her how to make *empanadas*. She depends on you."

The little girl's blue eyes zeroed in on his. He tried not to blink. After a minute, she crossed her arms. "You tell people things so they think they're getting something while you take something away."

Katie cracked up. "Out of the mouths of babes."

"Maybe she is ready for school after all," Jack said.

Later, when the kids were in bed, Jack and Katie sat on the couch as the lights danced on the bay. She was reading spreadsheets and he was Googling Frank Penny Sr. when his phone buzzed. Caller ID showed it was the landline at Hark's body shop.

"Speak," Jack answered.

"Uh, is this Jack?" a voice whispered. "Mr. McCoul?"

"Who's this?"

"It's Vinny. Remember me? I work for Hark."

"Why are you whispering?"

"Some *cabrón* is trying to break in."

"Did you call the cops?"

"And get rousted like Hark did? Fuck da police."

"Where's the guy now?"

"Still outside. I'm looking at him on a TV we got hooked to a camera shows the entrance and parking lot."

That was news to Jack. Hark's security system used to be nothing more than an alarm on the front door and a tire iron stashed behind the counter.

Vinny said, "It's not that I'm scared or anything. I'm no pussy. Just thought maybe if you drove by, he'd back off the front door so I could come out and kick his ass."

"I'm on my way. If he breaks in before I get there, hide."

TRAFFIC WAS light and Jack only challenged three red lights. He slowed as he neared Hark's. No one was creeping around the building as he drove past. He hung a U-turn and pulled into the parking lot. No one was ducking between the cars or hiding in the shadows of the building. He parked. No one rushed him or made a run for it. He called Vinny.

"I'm out front. Nobody's here."

"Yeah, I see you. Dude took his ass outta camera view a couple of minutes ago."

"Let me in so I can take a look around, check the back door and windows."

"Hang on."

Barrel locks slid and the steel front door screeched open. Vinny Vargas stood in the darkened entryway.

"Hit the shop lights, would you?" Jack said.

Banks of overhead fluorescents flickered and then bathed the room in cool white. Something glinted in Vinny's hand.

Jack squinted at the blade of a box cutter. "I think we're okay here."

"Oh, right. Sorry, man." He retracted the blade with the press of his thumb and slipped the cutter into the back pocket of his baggy jeans.

Jack made a circuit inside the shop. He opened the spray booth, checked the stock room, and yanked the door open to the bathroom. No one was hiding inside. The back door was securely locked and so were the windows in the front office.

"Does the video system have play back?" he asked.

"Yeah, but it only keeps about an hour's worth of recording before it records over itself. It's a cheap ass system mostly used for real time," Vinny said. "Should be long enough though."

He showed Jack where the monitor and recorder were kept.

Jack hit rewind, counted down a few minutes, and then hit play. Two cameras were hooked to the monitor and played on a split screen. One had a narrow field of view that focused on the approach to the front door. The other was wide angle and covered the parking lot. Jack and Vinny watched a static screen for a couple of minutes.

"There." Vinny pointed at a shadowy figure cutting into the lot from the sidewalk. "That's the dude. See, he's wearing a black hoody. Can't make out the brand of his shoes, but they look cheap as shit. Knock-offs you buy at KMart."

Jack glanced at Vinny's feet. He was wearing oversized white leather high tops with black laces, the pricey kind that punks beat each other up over.

The man in the hoody disappeared when he drew close to the building's steel roller bay door. He came back into view when he crossed into the range of the camera mounted above the front door.

"See, he's checking to see if it's locked," Vinny said. "Now he just stands there for a while. Then he's gonna stick his hands in his hoody. When I saw him do it for real, I'm thinking he's gonna pull out cannons and start spraying. Okay, a writer. I get it. I'm about to go out there and tell him to back off, but then watch what he does."

The man kept his face hidden. He pulled his hands out of the sweat shirt's pocket, put his fists together, and jabbed them at the camera like he was going to slug it. Jack hit the pause button. Tattooed letters showed on each finger below the first knuckle. LOCO was on the right. OCHO on the left.

"Crazy eight," Vinny said. "*Cabrón* is a banger, for sure, flashing signs like that. What's he want?"

"Recognition."

Jack froze the recording and took a picture of the knuckles with his phone. Afterwards, Vinny reset the device.

"You think he'll come back?"

"If he does, call me."

"Sure, but it's not like I can't handle him myself. I don't need no babysitter."

"No one said you did. Hark doesn't think so or else he wouldn't've trusted you to look after the place. Helping run the shop by day, guarding it at night."

The kid stuck out his chest. "True that. I ain't no punk."

"One thing I don't get though is, the night the cops stormed the place and arrested Hark, where were you?"

The look of pride drained from Vinny's face. "I don't know what you mean?"

"You being the night watchman and all, it sounds like you weren't even here or else you could've alibied Hark that he'd been here the whole time and couldn't've been on Osage where Frankie Jr. got beaten to death."

"It's not like that at all. I was—" He cut himself off.

Jack pounced. "Either you were here or you weren't. Can't be both. So, what was it?"

"I ain't saying."

"*Ain't* ain't an option." Jack drew up close. "Hark is not going down for something he didn't do. You read me?"

The kid flinched. "You going hit me?"

"No one's hitting anybody. Tell me what happened."

"That's just it. I don't know nothing. I was racking some heavy z's on account I'd worked all day and, okay, maybe I smoked a blunt and drank a couple of tall boys. I was out. I didn't hear nothing till later."

"I thought you slept on the couch in the front office."

"I did at first, but Hark set me up in my own room. Well, it's a storeroom in the back, but we cleared all the old stock out, parts and cans of paint and stuff, and put a cot in there. He said everybody deserves their own room. See, I never had one before."

"The cops bust down the front door and you don't hear anything?"

"My door was closed and I sleep with my buds on. When I do wake up and take 'em off, I hear all these voices. I'm thinking, like, we're getting jacked. I grab a cutter and open the door a crack. And there they are, the five-o leading Hark out in chains. Man, what am I s'posed to do?"

"Step out and say he'd been there all night, that's what."

Vinny shook his head. "Maybe, but I was holding. I got weed in the room and a case of Krylon colors and plus, well, plus I don't do cops."

"You got a record?"

"Maybe. Okay. Some small juvie shit. Nothing big."

"You a runaway?"

"From what? A mother who doesn't give a shit 'cause I'm the oldest mouth to feed among her five other brats? Besides..."

"Besides what?"

"The po-po hook me up to a lie detector test, what am I going say when they ask me if I can vouch for Hark? I don't know if he's been here all night or not. I could be the dude who puts him away by not saying he was. You understand?"

"I had to ask. We'll keep this between us, okay?"

"Sure, man." And Vinny stuck out a fist and they bumped.

## 15

A one-eyed seagull perched on the deck railing outside The Pier Inn and squawked at customers for french fries.

"Forget it. Junk food's bad for you," Jack said as he neared the front door.

Wonder Boy was at his usual station. He had a thick mug placed on the bar by the time Jack settled onto a stool.

"That seagull's going to take a bite out of someone," Jack said.

"It already has."

"You can't shoo it away?"

Wonder shrugged. "The animal rights people."

"Tell me about it. You know how Katie is. She'd bring it home, feed it fresh fish, and tuck it into bed."

"All creatures great and s-s-small."

"Including the two-legged kind. Speaking of, what have you heard about the big man?"

"You haven't s-s-spoken to Hark?"

"Later today. But I'm guessing you already have the 411."

Wonder Boy never acknowledged a compliment. He worked his rag into the already spotless bar.

"He was in a four-man cell but they moved him to s-s-solitary after an altercation in the chow line."

"Was it the usual push-and-shove stuff or something more?"

"There was no weapon, and when the guards broke it up, Hark and the other inmate s-s-said it was a s-s-simple case of accidentally bumping into each other when the line s-s-stopped."

"Of course they did. Did you find out if the guards wrote it up?"

"No."

"Because if so, the DA will use it as evidence of anger management issues at the prelim. No way Hark would get bail."

"I will s-s-see if it was put in his file."

"Okay, but on the QT. Hopefully, Broadshank will get him out of there before anything else happens." Jack worked on the cup of coffee. "I was checking out Frank Penny Sr. online last night, but something came up so I didn't get very far. What have you learned?"

"Frank Penny & S-S-Son has grown to become the largest commercial broker in the Mission District. They moved into building ownership and management. Their holdings include retail and apartment buildings as well as s-s-single family residences."

"Are they spread out all over the neighborhood or concentrated on Mission Street?"

"A rectangle between S-S-Sixteenth and Thirtieth and S-S-South Van Ness and Dolores."

"He avoids Pacific Heights and Sea View because wealthy tenants won't put up with bad plumbing and strong-arm collection tactics."

"The company is certainly no friend of the S-S-San Francisco Tenants Union."

"What landlord is? SFTU goes back to the sixties. It's got lots of pro bono lawyers on board to go along with their megaphones and picket signs. Do they have a specific beef with Penny?"

"S-s-supposedly there is an entire hard drive dedicated to tenant complaints about him."

"And nothing ever sticks, right?"

"Frank S-S-Senior is politically well connected."

"But you found a link between him and Supervisor Berlin, didn't you?"

Wonder Boy topped off Jack's mug. It was his way of smiling. "Campaign filings s-s-show he is the s-s-supervisor's s-s-single largest campaign contributor."

Jack pondered his mug. "Money and politics and power. The strongest cocktail there is."

The one-eyed seagull squawked so loud Jack turned around. "Sounds like I'm not the only one who thinks so."

"A s-s-seagull is actually one of the s-s-smartest of all birds. They have complex communication s-s-skills, use tools to open s-s-shellfish, and can drink s-s-salt water."

"Is that so? Maybe he knows how we can spring Hark. Tell you what. You rustle up an order of french fries and I'll go ask."

## 16

Broadshank, Hicklin, and Wong, LLP occupied the twentieth floor of one of San Francisco's oldest high-rises, a sand-colored building at the corner of Sutter and Montgomery. Its late Gothic Revival style put it on the National Register of Historic Places.

The law office's receptionist wore eyeliner and a fuchsia pantsuit. He greeted Jack with an air kiss. "Ooh, a three-day stubble to go along with your leather jacket and 501s. Very Outside meets GQ."

"Maybe I should borrow a tie if I'm going to pass myself off as part of CB's legal team," Jack said.

The receptionist giggled. "As if anyone at the Hall doesn't already know who you are. Go on back, cover boy. He's expecting you."

Broadshank had a corner suite with windows that provided a glimpse of the bay between a forest of newly built skyscrapers.

"Jack, my boy. We have a few minutes before we need to depart. Perhaps we should go over recent events."

The corpulent counselor was lodged behind a desk that once

served as a dining table at The Old Poodle Dog, a French restaurant whose doors had closed decades before but with roots going back to the Gold Rush. Framed menus from Michelin-starred restaurants autographed by their celebrity chefs festooned the walls.

"Okay, for starters, what about this so-called witness who says he overheard Hark and Frankie arguing. Ricky Udo is employed by Frank Sr.?"

"Naturally, I shall seek to discredit Mr. Udo in a cross-examination during a trial, but a preliminary hearing is another matter."

"We can't let it get to trial."

"That is understood."

"And what about this? Frank Penny Sr. is Supervisor Berlin's single largest campaign contributor. Berlin is suddenly all about using Hark's arrest as a symbol for his law and order platform. Isn't that some kind of conflict of interest?"

Broadshank leaned back and twiddled his thumbs. "Supervisor Berlin's receipt of campaign donations from the father of the man Mr. Martinez allegedly murdered is not illegal. I would be very hard pressed to use that as a defense."

"Even if we found out Berlin is only doing it because Frank Sr. is pulling his strings?"

"Let us agree to leave the defense strategy to me, my boy. Any influence Mr. Penny has over the supervisor will likely be short-lived once Mr. Berlin becomes mayor. I am told he believes he is destined for greatness beyond San Francisco. Surely, he has eyes on becoming governor one day. Who knows? Maybe even president. The supervisor is indubitably convinced the means for achieving such position of power are justified no matter what that may entail."

"Meaning Machiavelli isn't one of the Three Tenors."

Broadshank's guffaw was as stentorious as his courtroom

delivery. "Good one, my boy. I had forgotten your tenure at parochial school included a classics education."

"*Veni, vidi, vici.* That one I learned on the street of hard knocks."

"The question remains, though, how does a connection between Messieurs Penny and Berlin have anything to do with the crime that my client has been charged with? That is what I will be asked should I allege it during the preliminary hearing or in trial."

"I'm not sure, but my gut tells me there's something there. What, exactly, is something we need to find out."

"I am afraid that is the responsibility of the police."

"They've already made up their minds. It's up to me to change them. I owe it to Hark."

"Certainly, my boy. And all within the confines of the law so that we do nothing to further jeopardize his case, would not you agree?"

"Understood. Any chance the prelim will overturn Cowboy Chun's denial of bail?"

"Slim and none and both are fasting." Broadshank shuddered at the very thought of missing a meal.

"So we keep a full-court press to show he's innocent."

"Of course, but I must warn you Mr. Martinez could remain incarcerated for a year or more before the matter even comes to trial should the judge rule there is probable cause for a murder trial. The district attorney can either speed or delay a juried trial."

"She's running for reelection too. What you're saying is, why risk a loss if you're running as a winner."

"Precisely."

When Broadshank uttered it he began swaying. A feeling of queasiness washed over Jack as he watched. And then he realized he was moving too. The framed menus tilted like dog heads. The building pitched.

"Earthquake!" Jack shouted.

"My god!" Broadshank thundered. He put both hands on the heavy desk to brace himself.

Jack considered diving underneath it. While the old building's windows were small compared to the new steel and glass towers blooming throughout downtown, the shards would still be lethal if they started flying. A quake larger than an 8.0 would leave the financial district's streets covered in drifts of broken glass six feet deep.

As quickly as it had started, the swaying stopped.

"That had to have been in the fives," Broadshank pronounced as the bloom returned to his copious jowls.

"I'd wager somewhere in the middle."

Accuracy in estimating earthquake magnitude was as much a sport in San Francisco as betting on the outcomes of Giants games.

"Part of the price we pay to live in the most culinary vibrant community in the country," the lawyer said. "Alas, I am sure this temblor did not stop the wheels of justice from turning. Come, my driver awaits."

HARK SPORTED a cut on his chin and a bruise below his eye. Jack bet the other guy looked a helluva lot worse.

They were seated in a windowless room. Hark was handcuffed to a thick eye hook bolted to the middle of a table etched with profanities. Broadshank had spread a handkerchief on his chair before sitting. Jack made a note to wash his jeans as soon as he got home.

"We're working flat out and full tilt to get you out," he said to Hark.

The big man didn't show a reaction. His eyes were flat, his face void. It's what experienced cons did as soon as the cell door slammed behind them. Looking sidewise at the wrong person could be fatal. Hark had done a couple of minor stints in lockup when he was a young banger. A serious charge that would've sent him to Stockton Correctional for a long jolt got dropped when the public defender traded it for Hark's consent to enlist in the army.

A guard stood a few paces behind. He gripped a telescopic steel baton. Broadshank waved a cautionary finger at Hark.

"It is incumbent upon me to advise everyone present that this conversation is protected by attorney-client privilege and is confidential and undiscoverable under all pertinent laws and regulations. Anything said is inadmissible in a court of law and in no way can be construed as evidentiary. Despite the all-encompassing legal protection afforded by such privilege, I hereby acknowledge to my client that I cannot guarantee the privacy of this locale as the presence of a uniformed sheriff's deputy compromises it. Therefore, our conversation must be restricted in frankness."

"You must get paid by the word," Hark muttered.

"CB's the best suit there is," Jack said. "Let him do his job."

Hark didn't apologize. If he did, chances were the guard would trade the info to the wolves on the block who'd view it as a sign of weakness.

"What do I need to know for the prelim besides *Not* and *Guilty*?" he asked.

"Nothing more," Broadshank said. "I shall speak on your behalf."

"They're not going give me bail until then?"

"My office is working on that very issue. But I must advise

you it would be highly unlikely to achieve a satisfactory outcome prior to the preliminary hearing. You can be assured I shall argue for it most vociferously."

Hark looked at his wrist. The handcuff had bitten deep into his flesh. He leaned forward. "Any chance they'll send me to San Bruno before then?"

San Bruno was ten miles south and San Francisco's newest prison. Like the jails on the top floors of the Hall of Justice, the San Francisco Sheriff's Department managed it despite the fact it was just over the line in San Mateo County. Jailhouse scuttle-butt was rife with stories about prisoners awaiting trial being sent to San Bruno and getting lost in the system, both purposely and accidentally.

Broadshank's voice rose with conviction. "That would be a serious miscarriage of justice and one that I shall make a priority to prevent from occurring."

The guard slapped the baton in his palm. "Time's up. Let's go."

Jack said, "Wait a sec. We have something he needs to see."

The guard pointed the steel stick at Jack. "You pass the prisoner anything you'll land in the cell next to him."

Jack squared his jaw. "Civil Code 28678 states that a prisoner who is being held but not convicted cannot be denied the ability to manage his legitimate business affairs. I have a paper here that requires his attention."

"Forget it. He's not getting his hands on a pen to sign anything. He gets nothing he can turn into a shiv or crack pipe."

"He doesn't need to sign it."

Before the guard had time to make another objection, Jack slid a folder toward Hark. "Vinny had a question about a customer. Guy came in for a special paint job. Some kind of design. Vinny lost the paperwork. Thought you might know how to contact the customer."

Jack flipped the folder open. It contained a screen shot of the tattooed fists spelling out LOCO OCHO.

Hark studied it. "Don't know him offhand. I'd need my book, but since I don't got it with me, ask Rosa. If anybody knows, she would."

The guard took a step closer to look over Hark's shoulder. "What is that?"

Jack closed the folder and snatched it back. "Proprietary business information protected by more rules and regulations than I have time to recite."

The guard's lips twisted into a snarl. "Lawyers. You're all the same."

Jack didn't take the bait. He said to Hark, "Vinny's doing a good job minding the store while you're here."

"He's a good kid. A born natural sprayer."

"He must be living off the food trucks that park out front because he never leaves the place."

"Doing his job."

"We talked, you know, about his room in the back. He's still sleeping good, you know? All through the night like before."

Hark's nod said the message was received loud and clear. "And it stays that way. Leave it alone, *ese*. Don't pick at it."

Jack wanted to argue the kid could be his ticket out, but Hark must have his reasons for playing it the way he was. "I won't," he said.

Hark jerked his manacled wrist and called to the guard. "We're done here."

The guard unlocked Hark from the eye hook. "Let's go."

Jack said, "Watch your back."

Hark grinned. "I learned a long time ago not to pick a bar of soap off the floor."

Down on the street, Broadshank said, "That civil code number you quoted is utter nonsense."

"I know, but the guard didn't."

"And what was all that about the young man who is staying at Mr. Martinez's. I was counting on him to provide my client with an alibi."

"He can't," Jack said.

"*Can't*? My interpretation of your recent dialogue with Mr. Martinez was that he is not being allowed to. Is that your wish or my client's?"

"We have to find another way. Vinny's a dead end."

Broadshank tut-tutted. "I cannot do my job if critical information that could have a significant bearing on the case is withheld from me."

"Weren't you the one who once told me plausible deniability is one of the best tools in a defense lawyer's arsenal?"

The lawyer paused. "Quite right. Now I really must be going. We shall reconnoiter in the morning."

## 17

The lunch crowd had thinned by the time Jack arrived at Abuelita's Restaurant. A couple were lingering over margaritas in a corner booth. Three men dressed in PG&E uniforms mopped up *chile verde* sauce with tortillas. A busboy cleared a table.

Hark's grandmother was in the kitchen hovering over the stove. She stirred an enormous pot of pinto beans with a silver ladle. Sliced *poblanos* roasted in a cast iron skillet.

Jack greeted her by saying, "*Buenos tardes.*"

Her smile flashed gold. "*¿Tienes hambre? Siéntate y te traeré una placa.*"

Jack wasn't hungry but he sat at the kitchen counter as instructed. She filled a bowl with beans, sprinkled shredded cheese and fresh cilantro on top, and slid a couple of the blackened peppers on a dish.

He took a few bites. "*Delicioso, Abuelita. Que sabrosa.*"

The old lady beamed. She was the picture of a kind and loving grandmother—an *abuelita*. It was why everyone called her that and why her restaurant was named that. Hark and Jack were among a handful who knew her given name. If the room at the jail had been bugged—and odds were it was—the cops would have a hard time tracking down anyone named Rosa.

Jack finished the bowl under her watchful eye and then slipped the photo out of the folder and showed it to her.

"*¿Alguna vez ha visto estos antes?*" he asked.

The smile melted from her lips when she saw the tattooed knuckles. Her shoulders sagged and eyes glistened.

"You know who it is, don't you? *¿Conoces al hombre?*"

She returned to the stove and resumed stirring the pot of beans.

Jack said, "It's okay. You can tell me. It might help free Hark."

The old woman banged the ladle on the edge of the pot to shake off any beans and then started firing away in rapid Spanish. Jack had to work at it to keep up. The man was named Benicio Tuxtla. He'd grown up in the Mission District and belonged to a street gang. He'd been her daughter's boyfriend at one time. The old lady had always disapproved of him. Tuxtla was rough and ran with a dangerous crowd. Her daughter was only a teenager. No matter how hard she tried, she couldn't break the pair apart. Tuxtla eventually took a fall for murdering a rival and was sentenced to life in Folsom. Nobody had heard from him since.

Jack thought on it and wondered why Tuxtla would go out of his way to signal his presence to Hark. He asked her if Tuxtla was locked up before or after Hark was born.

"*Antes de.*"

*Before.* Her tone left no doubt, but Jack knew it didn't rule Tuxtla out as Hark's father. He sucked his teeth and then asked her directly.

She swung around and waved the ladle at him. "*No. Nunca. Él no es su padre.*" She banged it on the counter. "*Él es el diablo.*"

Jack had never seen her so upset before, but her anger raised more questions than answers. Tuxtla might be the devil, all right, but he might also be Hark's dad. Jack started to ask if her daughter ever mentioned him to Hark before she split for L.A., but seeing the old woman in pain made the decision to swallow the question easy.

He patted her on the shoulder "*No te preocupes, abuelita. Todo estará bien.*"

"What's going to be okay?" a voice piped from the doorway.

It was Zita. Katie was there too. She held Harry.

Jack swooped up Zita and gave her a hug in hopes of heading off any more questions. "What a surprise. Are you here to make *empanadas*?"

The old woman's smile returned. She reached into a basket and pulled out a fresh-baked Mexican wedding cookie. In seconds Zita's fingers and lips were covered with powdered sugar.

Katie passed Harry to Jack. "I'm glad you're here. I was going to ask if she could look after the kids while I run over to the Bayview gym. A pipe burst and water's gushing everywhere."

"You want me to go instead?"

"It's better if I do. There will be rescheduling issues to deal with and a million other things. Let's divide and conquer. I was on my way to the grocery store when I got the call. Why don't you take the car and kids and pick up something for dinner? I'll grab a Lyft and see you later."

And before he could agree, she flipped him the car keys and was gone.

## 18

The Whole Foods on Eighteenth and Rhode Island was on the way home. Jack parked in the underground garage, settled Harry into a backpack, and commandeered a shopping cart. With Zita serving as guide, they mushed up and down the aisles.

The little girl clapped her hands when they reached the produce section. "Pumpkins. I want *carbonada en zapallo*."

"What's that?" Jack asked.

She rolled her eyes. "*Tu hablas Espanol*."

"I hear *carbonara*, I think Italian pasta."

"*Carbonada*." Again, a roll of her blue eyes. "It's stew made in a *zapallo*."

"Sounds like a Cinderella story. Instead of a coach, the pumpkin turns into a pot."

"Fairy tales are for babies."

Jack gave her a look. "How old are you, again? Like, a teenager?"

"I used to eat it all the time until you took me away."

Jack knew troubled water when he saw it, so he treaded carefully. "I brought you to San Francisco because I'm your father. I needed to keep you safe. Because..." He took a breath. "Because I love you, *mija*."

She crossed her arms.

Jack patted her head. "Okay, you pick out a big, fat pumpkin and I'll grab the veggies."

They loaded everything into the cart, and after a quick spin down the frozen aisle for a pint of pistachio ice cream, made their way through the checkout line.

Jack nosed the cart against the car to keep it from rolling away on its own, hoisted Harry out of the backpack, and set to work buckling the infant into a car seat. Fastening the straps required him to hunch over the back seat. Harry started to fuss.

"Jack," Zita said.

"I'm doing it as fast as I can. You're next."

"But Jack."

"Hang on a sec."

"Papa," she said.

Zita never called him that. With his radar pinging, he cranked around to see what the problem was.

"Papa!" she cried.

Ricky Udo had his hand on Zita's shoulder. His blond goatee added an obscene circle to his leer. "I didn't know you was a mommy daddy."

"Get away from my daughter."

Udo gripped Zita's shoulder with his left hand and shoved his right hand into the pocket of his Raiders jacket. A gun barrel turned the fabric into a pup tent.

"Whoa, partner. You don't want to scare this sweet little thing." His leer widened.

"What do you want?"

"That's more like it. Nice and friendly."

"I said, what do you want?"

"I hear your boy is bobbing for apples in the can. Serves him right for what he did to Frank Jr. He's going to the row. They got him dead to rights."

"Pretty convenient you being the witness."

The leer turned into a grin. "Just doing my citizenly duty."

"What about your babysitting duty?"

"I don't know what you're babbling about."

"I never took Frank Sr. for the kind to condone dereliction of duty. Especially when it came to protecting Junior."

"Nobody derelicted nothing."

"So where were you when Frankie stepped into Osage Alley?"

"You're talking in circles again."

"Am I?"

Udo scrunched his face. "The way I heard it, you think you're some kind of hot shot when it comes to beating the odds, but you know what I think? I think I could beat you with one hand tied behind my back." He mimicked a boxer's footwork.

"The only thing you should be thinking right now is what'll happen if you don't let go of my daughter."

"I think you don't count odds so good." Udo poked the gun against his pocket harder.

Seeing Zita touched by a punk like Ricky Udo made Jack wish he did pack a gun. He wouldn't think twice. Udo's gun was pointed at him, not his daughter. He'd draw and put one dead center in that filthy goatee. No matter if he took a slug himself in the exchange. No matter if it brought Terry Dolan and all the cops in San Francisco down on him. No matter if killing a man would send him to prison forever.

The blood was rushing hot and fast through his veins. It sent his heart thumping against his chest so hard he was sure his shirt was billowing. Every nerve ending from his toes to his head was on fire.

Zita must've sensed it. Her lips quivered. Her eyes pooled. And then she started to shake. She shook so hard it was like she was having a convulsion.

Udo lurched backwards as if the little girl was contagious. "What the fuck?"

It was all the opening Jack needed. He rushed in and tore Zita away from Ricky Udo's grip, spun her around, and blocked her body with his own. He half expected to hear an explosion. Feel the burn of a slug tearing through his back. He pushed Zita into the backseat and slammed the door.

When he turned around, Udo was laughing. "What I thought. A fuckin' mommy daddy." He spit at Jack's feet and swaggered away.

Jack's blood was still racing. He yanked a cloth shopping bag out of the cart and pulled a potato from it. The spud was the size of a baseball. When he played shortstop, he could throw out a runner heading for home no problem. He reared back and fired. Jack didn't wait to see if he hit Udo or not. He was already sprinting after him, the cloth bag swinging by its straps. Udo stumbled when the potato struck him between the shoulder blades. He threw out his hands to break his fall against a parked car. Jack was on him in a flash, swinging the bag full of spuds, pummeling the punk's ribs and shoulders.

Udo swore.

Jack kept swinging. "Whose Mr. Fight Club now?"

When Udo covered his head, Jack kneed him in the crotch, reached into his Raiders jacket pocket, and fished out a black 9mm.

He screwed the barrel into Udo's ear. "You ever get near my kids again, I'll empty every round into your skull."

Jack shoved the gun into his own waistband and turned around. A couple of people were staring at him, frozen behind their shopping carts.

He flashed them an aw-shucks grin. "Nothing to worry about here folks. Just a little misunderstanding about the last jar of artichoke hearts on the shelf."

Wide-eyed stares followed him as he got in the Prius and drove away.

## 19

Zita and Harry were playing in their bedroom. The smell of cooked pumpkin filled the air, and dirty dishes were piled in the sink. Jack sat at the dining table and worked on a double Jameson. Neat. Cooking and eating dinner with the kids had a calming effect after the run-in with Udo. The whisky was helping it stay that way.

Even so, his thoughts kept picking at the edges of what might've happened in the garage. Rage, revenge, and remorse ranked high among man's worst enemies. Unchecked, they ran amok like cancer, sure to eat away body and soul. Jack never questioned he would always protect the ones he loved, but up until now he'd always been able to use his wits to save someone in need, whether by staging a simple sleight of hand or executing a complex long con.

Sure, he'd never hesitated to throw a punch or two when circumstances warranted, even rely on Hark who had a practical approach to applying lethal force when all else failed. But after teetering on the brink of homicide, he realized the tenets of his moral code weren't as unshakable as he thought. Fatherhood hadn't dulled his edge. It made it even sharper.

A buzz snapped his introspection. An app linked his phone to the intercom at the security gate on the street. Katie had called earlier to say the mess at the gym was worse than expected and not to hold dinner for her. *She must've forgotten the numbered code to access the lobby and elevator again*, he thought. Such was the way of life with so many PINs and passwords to remember.

He answered the phone by saying, "Our anniversary. Day, month, year."

"I wouldn't know. I wasn't there," Detective Terry Dolan replied. "Buzz me in. We need to talk."

Jack showed no surprise. "About what?"

"I'll tell you in person."

"Sounds official."

"It will be if you make it that way."

"Maybe I better call Broadshank."

"Don't be a dumbass. Let me in."

Terry Dolan had been a choir boy all through St. Joseph's. Hearing him swear was as out of the ordinary as Zita calling him *Papa*. Jack hit the buzzer, downed the rest of his Jameson, and considered his options while waiting for the homicide cop to reach the fourth floor.

He was glad to see Terry wasn't backed by a uniformed officer or two. And he wasn't holding out an arrest warrant either. The detective was wearing his trademark blue suit, but his tie was loosened and the top button undone. There was something else different about him. The air of self-confidence he'd cultivated since school days was missing.

"You look like you could use a drink," Jack said.

Terry waved him off. He was as abstemious as a vegan visiting a McDonald's, a legacy of having a drunk policeman for a dad. That was one of the few things they had in common.

"Okay, tea it is," Jack said. "Katie keeps plenty of herb blends around. Cactus spine. Burnt oak leaves. Old kale and carrot tops. What'll it be?"

Either Terry didn't hear him or failed to register the joke. He gestured to the table. "Mind?"

"Take a load off. I'll put the kettle on."

Jack returned with a cup and slid it in front of him. "Why are you here?"

Terry ignored the tea. "I saw a report about two men fighting in a Whole Foods parking lot."

"Let me guess. Two bums playing tug-of-war over a sack full of beer cans they'd filched from the recycling bin."

"The report describes one of them racing away in a Prius. It gave a partial on the plate."

"There's your problem right there. Unreliable witness. You ever hear of a Prius that could race anywhere?"

"The suspect had two children in the backseat. You match the description."

"I once saw a news story about these women battling it out at Walmart on Black Friday." Jack mocked a shudder. "I've done all my shopping online ever since."

Terry glared. Jack returned it. They went eyeball-to-eyeball for a while. Jack blew on his teacup even though it was filled with whisky.

"Come on, Terry," he finally said. "Sharp-elbowed shoppers aren't your beat. What do you really want?"

It took him another minute to work up to it. "It's the Garza case. The captain gave me a full five minutes of what ho. He said the chief had given the same to him. 'Get your people in line, he said.' He being the chief. Me being the people."

"So, go out and round up the usual suspects. Show the brass you're busting ass. You're good at that."

"It's the other way around. They want me to go slow. I'm not getting any resources. Garza's body? The pathologist is suddenly overwhelmed with higher priorities. The evidence the CSI team tagged and bagged at the scene? The findings are on back order."

"Sounds like typical bureaucracy to me."

"Garza had security cameras," Terry continued. "The doers knew where they were because they spray painted the lenses. There is software out now that lets you see through paint. It's some kind of new digitizing technique. Only all of a sudden, the recordings from the cameras got *misplaced*. I was told they probably had the wrong label slapped on them and shipped to off-site storage. Do you know how large that warehouse is?"

He picked up the teacup, took a drink, and made a face.

Jack said, "I warned you. You ought to get a whiff of her homemade first aid ointment. Smells like a sock that needs washing."

Terry swallowed, only it wasn't tea going down his throat. "Don't make this harder than it already is. I've never complained about the job once. I've never gone outside the house to ask for help in my life."

"I'm flattered. Really. So, what do you want from me?"

"I'm getting nowhere with the neighborhood canvas. Maybe people have said something to you because you're a—"

"Law-abiding citizen who pays his taxes, supports public radio, and donates to SF Jazz? That kind of person, you mean."

Terry choked down some more pride. "I'd appreciate it if you let me know what you've heard. If you don't have anything, maybe you could ask around."

"What you really want to be saying is, 'Jack, old chum, you were absolutely right when you told me Garza's murder has to do with a landlord beef and Supervisor Berlin is throwing me under the cable car.' "

"I looked into the landlord angle. Nothing panned out."

"Maybe you didn't look hard enough."

"And I still don't see why Berlin cares about my investigation."

"He wouldn't be the first politician to use crime to win an election. Scare the shit out of the voters that the cops aren't doing their job and then offer yourself as the law-and-order ticket."

"What does that have to do with the chief ordering me to take my foot off the gas?"

"Maybe the chief conducted his own election poll and realized it pays to make nice with Berlin now so the first time the department's budget goes up for review, the new mayor will keep his shears holstered."

Terry slid his teacup around. "That's pretty cynical."

" 'Cynicism is an unpleasant way of saying the truth.' Lillian Hellman said that."

"Tiptoeing around a politician doesn't get me any closer to finding out who killed Garza."

"You said you looked into the landlord angle. You found nothing?"

"Garza had filed some plain vanilla complaints about breaches to the lease—bad maintenance, rent increases. Things like that. And there's a phone record of him saying he'd been harassed, but nothing came of it. None of it stacks up to the fact that his safe was emptied."

"Except that Frank Penny & Son Real Estate was Garza's landlord. And the son part of same company was murdered shortly thereafter."

Terry threw up his hands. "There's nothing to tie the two killings. One was most likely a robbery. The other an assault and battery."

"Hark didn't do it."

"So you say, but that's in the district attorney's hands now. I'm focused on Garza."

"But why aren't the police investigating Frankie's death?"

"Because the DA is pretty sure she's got her man."

"Jeez, Terry. You're asking me for help, but no *quid pro quo*?"

"What can I do? I've been off the Penny case since they put Hark in the box."

"Who wanted to stop a full investigation?"

"Who says anybody did? Maybe their case is solid."

"And maybe Berlin wants two unsolveds to spotlight his law and order platform. Maybe the DA doesn't want Penny's murder investigated because she could run the risk of having the arrest thrown out before her own election."

"Do you really believe Frank Penny Sr. isn't lighting a fire under the DA and police commission to put his son's killer away as quickly as possible? Frank Jr. meant everything to him."

"Unless it pays him to be patient."

"And how does that work?"

"The three principles of real estate have always been location, location, location, but in San Francisco, it's also connection, connection, connection. A homeowner can't even put up a swing set in the backyard without getting a permit first. You got your planning commission, your building inspector, your health and safety people. You name it, there's a department with somebody's hand out."

"What does that have to do with Frank Jr.'s murder investigation?"

"What if Frank Sr. has ensured his company's future by locking arms with the ultimate permitter?"

"You mean Berlin if he wins."

"Penny's on record as being one of his biggest campaign contributors."

"So are lots of other developers. So are a lot of tech companies. Guess what? They all play both sides of the fence during campaign season to hedge their bets."

"But what if there's more?"

"More what? Penny promising payoffs for building permits? That seems pretty small change for one of the wealthiest landlords in the city."

"Remember Boss Tweed? He made millions through redevelopment projects by passing ordinances and stacking the government with other crooked officials. What if Berlin wires it the same way? If he wins the mayor's seat, he'll have a license to print money. Especially if he cooks up some kind of new earthquake law that lets him condemn entire blocks of buildings and then green-lights huge redevelopment projects for pals like Frank Penny to build."

Terry shoved his teacup aside. "You're a con man, Jack. That's something you would do. Berlin is the poster child of civic responsibility and champion of the underserved."

"That's not a bad cover."

"Coming here was a mistake. I trust you'll keep this conversation just between us."

"No worries. I got my own reputation to think of."

Zita ran into the room, but stopped short when she saw Terry. "Oh, hello."

"Hello to you too," he said.

Jack said, "This is Detective Dolan. He's a policeman."

"Is he your friend?" Zita asked Jack.

"We went to school together."

"But doesn't that make him your friend? When I go to school, won't the other boys and girls be my friends too?"

"Sure they will."

"So then, you two are friends."

Jack shot a glance at Terry, but kept silent.

Zita said, "If you're Jack's friend, then you can be my friend too. I'm Zita."

"That's a pretty name," he said.

"It means little girl. *Naci en Argentina*."

Terry searched for a response, but a squall sounded from the kids' bedroom.

Jack said, "Doodie calls."

He changed Harry and brought him out. "And this is Harry. Harry, say hello to Terry."

The baby burped.

Jack said, "Don't take it personal."

Terry seemed stunned by the infant's presence. "I have to go," he mumbled.

Jack, cradling the baby, opened the door.

Terry stared at Harry again. He reached over and laid his palm against the baby's face. "He sure has Katie's features. Tell her I said so, okay? Tell her I said, well, tell her congratulations."

As he walked down the darkened hall toward the elevator, Jack almost felt sorry for him.

## 20

It was shortly before nine in the morning and rancheria music was already pouring from the open cavities of a building on Mission Street that was undergoing a major facelift. Hardhats wearing brown Carhartt bib overalls and tool belts clambered on a bridgework of scaffolding. Jack avoided getting run over by a forklift delivering a pallet of drywall. The building was a used furniture store when he was growing up. He remembered his father stalking out of it when a salesman wouldn't come down on the price of a beat-up bunkbed that would've freed some space in the cramped bedroom Jack shared with his two brothers.

He was entering the stairwell to his office when the echo of heavy footsteps signaled someone coming down. It was DD Mitchell.

"Something I can help you with?" Jack said.

The bar owner tried to brush past. "No. I'm good."

Jack didn't get out of his way. "Since I own the building, mind telling me what you're doing here?"

"Checking on an employee. Make sure she's okay and all. You know, after everything that's been going down."

"That employee being Valentine Song, you being a considerate boss and all."

"What's that supposed to mean?"

"What it sounds like. Why, is there anything more to it?"

"Piss off, McCoul. I don't got time for this." He shouldered his way past, jaywalked across the street, and disappeared into the Double Dice.

Jack took the stairs two at a time and knocked on Valentine's door. She was wearing a sarong and a smile which soon melted.

"Oh, hello." Her eyes darted to see around him.

"I ran into DD on his way out. He seems happy. I didn't know you two were an item."

The smile came back. Her teeth were as white as coconut milk. "He told you that? He so sweet."

"Yeah, a regular honey bear."

"Is it problem he spend night here? I not remember if it say so on rental agreement. I can pay more money."

"No, it's fine. I'm happy for you both."

"Me too. I like having boyfriend. DD so big and strong. I been little frightened because people got killed."

"Mind if I ask you something about that?"

"If I can help, okay, but I not know what I not know. I already told you I not see anything at Mr. Garza's store and I not there when Mr. Penny was beat up."

"I'm wondering if you've heard anything since then. Maybe someone from the neighborhood told you something or you overhead something while you were at work."

"Oh yes, but I not hear anything."

She reached for her hair and combed it with her fingers.

Jack said, "What about see anything?"

"I am not sure I understand."

"What did you see the night Frankie Penny was killed?"

"Why you say I saw anything?"

"When you're dancing at the Gold Rush, can you tell when someone wants to give you a big tip before they do it?"

"That easy. They hold up bills. I dance close and they fold them in my G-string."

"But before they hold out any money. Do you see something that tells you they're likely to tip even if they're bashful?"

"Oh yes, I understand now. Some men look with their head down. Other men peel label off beer bottle but they really looking at me. Biggest tippers are men who pretend not look at all."

"Those signs are called a *tell*. The same in poker when someone's bluffing. Everyone has a tell. You too. Yours is playing with your hair."

"I do that? I did not know."

"You saw something that night. Tell me and I can help you."

"But I am frightened."

"Because of what you saw."

"I not want trouble."

"Why would you get in trouble?"

"I want to stay in San Francisco. You understand? I like it here. I make money and send to my mother. I go to computer school, and one day I not need take clothes off. I get a big job and work at Facebook. Now I have boyfriend. Maybe we get married. If I make trouble they send me back, okay?"

"No one is going to send you anywhere. What did you see?"

Valentine bowed and shifted her weight. She was barefoot. Her toenails were bright red. The color was garish compared to the pastel butterflies that fluttered on her sarong.

"I saw men in parked car. From my window here." She swung her arm back to gesture. It made her sarong fall open. "When Mr. Penny came out of Double Dice they get out and talk to him."

"Was one of them Ricky Udo?"

"No."

"Who then?"

"It dark. I not see their faces."

"What happened after they stopped Frankie?"

"They talk and then they walk away."

"Frankie and them? Toward Osage Alley?"

"Oh yes, all three. Maybe they went there. Maybe not. I cannot see alley from window. Look yourself."

Jack did. The view to the corner was blocked.

"Am I in trouble? I like San Francisco. I like school. I like DD."

"Have you told anyone else?"

"No."

"Not even DD?"

"No. I not want make trouble for him either."

"Keep it that way, okay? Don't tell anyone unless I ask you to."

"Okay. I understand. Bye-bye, Jack. You the best. I get ready now for work at Gold Rush."

JACK WAS SEARCHING the Net for anything on the Pennys when Sami Alfassi rapped on his door. He smelled of cigarettes.

"I have your rent money." He extracted an envelope from his breast pocket and placed it on the desk. Jack's name was printed on the front in English, but the ascenders and descenders had Arabic flourishes. "It is all there. Please count it in front of me so there is no misunderstanding."

Jack didn't touch it. "I don't need to. Like I told you before, we can set up direct deposit so you don't have to carry cash."

"That is most considerate, but I prefer to transact my business this way. I have seen banks disappear overnight."

Jack was not about to argue the point. Truth was, he preferred cash too. The only bank he truly trusted was one in the Cayman Islands where he kept a numbered account and had a man on the inside.

Alfassi didn't seem to be in a hurry to leave. Jack took the cue and pointed to a chair.

"How is your son and daughter?" he began.

"They are as well as can be expected, *Al-ḥamdu lillāh*. And your children?"

"They keep me young, but make me old."

"It is the same for all fathers, is it not?"

They talked about the weather and sports. Alfassi said he preferred soccer. Jack asked if he followed the San Jose Earthquakes. Alfassi said from time to time, but his favorite team was a French club from Marseille.

"Not a Syrian team?" Jack said.

"My country is at war. Football players are the age of soldiers. Most are dead."

Jack ran a hand across his jaw. "The most dangerous thing teams face here is a wardrobe malfunction during the half-time show."

"I do not understand."

"Frankly, neither do I. Look, okay if I change the subject?"

"You wish to discuss Mr. Garza's murder," Alfassi said.

The man's intuition or directness no longer surprised Jack. "Yeah, and Frank Penny Jr.'s too. I'm digging around trying to find answers. Have you heard anything?"

"The killings are of concern to all and, of course, the subject of speculation and gossip. Many shopkeepers meet regularly to discuss them. Not in public, but in the back rooms of cafés after they have closed for the night."

"What are they saying?" Jack said.

"Most believe the murder of Mr. Garza was not the result of a robbery. Threats against tenants have continued. Three store owners have been assaulted in the past two days."

"And like before, no one's called the cops."

"It is a matter of trust. Most shopkeepers prefer to be self-reliant."

"If that means keeping a gun behind the counter, then they should reconsider. The odds of getting the drop on a robber before getting shot is a sucker's bet since a gun is already pointed in their face. And since what we're really talking about here is paid professional muscle hassling them, then the odds are even worse. A shopkeeper may be able to chase the heavies off, but sure as beer is beer no matter what fancy label they slap on the bottle, they'll come right back. And when they do, they'll be carrying a lot more firepower."

"I have seen what happens when law and order breaks down. There are no winners, only survivors."

"What do you propose they do about it?"

"I am advocating taking the issue to the media to bring pressure on the government to protect shopkeepers from the interests that are seeking to drive us out."

"A solid plan. You'll need a mouthpiece, though. That's the way it works here."

"I believe you call it a spokesperson."

"Exactly."

"I doubt we could find a public relations agency with the courage to go against such powerful interests. And then there is the question of money. We could never pay what the real estate interests can afford."

"You shouldn't pay anybody anything. It's much better if you don't use some overpaid flack. That just makes you look the same as the guys you're trying to beat. A real person, a real shopkeeper who's getting squeezed, makes for a better story. It's the little guy versus the big guy."

"David and Goliath." When Jack looked surprised, Alfassi smiled. "Yes, the Qur'an contains a similar passage."

"There's always a big bully needs taking down, don't you know?"

"There is an obstacle to your David strategy," the shopkeeper said. "English is not the first language of many who are being victimized. Few, if any, have experience speaking to the press."

"What about you? A hardworking single father trying to make a better life for his family? The media would eat that up."

Alfassi touched his forehead. "Alas, that is not my destiny."

"Why not?"

"I do not have a landlord who is mistreating me." He touched his forehead and then held his hand palm up toward Jack.

"Okay, why don't you keep your eye out and see if maybe there isn't somebody else who fits the bill. In the meantime, the shopkeepers who were recently beat up, can they describe the guys who did it?"

"But of course. Everyone can. The men have been doing so with impunity for so long now that they do not bother to hide their faces. The leader is the most brazen. He is named Udo. They say he is a boxer."

"He's a punk. Nothing more," Jack said.

"You know him?"

"I've run into him."

"He is employed by a very powerful man."

"Frank Penny Sr."

"The same. And since it was his son who was murdered, shopkeepers are more fearful than ever. Many come from places where a father is not only honor-bound to avenge his son's death, but may do so without fear of legal retribution."

Jack sucked his teeth. "Have you ever had a run-in with Ricky Udo? Or either of the Pennys, son or father?"

"No. I only know the father by his reputation. He owns several of the buildings on Mission Street, including the one down the street now undergoing rehabilitation. It is no secret he desires to transform the entire neighborhood."

"Supervisor Berlin would say what Penny is doing is good for the city."

"And could it also be said that it is good for Mr. Berlin as well?"

"Well, well, well. Can't pull the wool over your eyes."

"One does not need to come from a poor agricultural country like mine to recognize a wolf in sheep's clothing."

"You're a smart man, Alfassi. You sure you don't want to lead the shopkeepers' charge?"

"Alas, not." He shrugged. "May I ask you something?"

Jack said, "Fire away."

"Do you think this Ricky Udo killed Mr. Garza?"

"I don't know."

"And what about Mr. Penny's son? Are the two crimes related?"

"I'm coming up empty on that one too, but I'm looking into it."

"Why? You are not with law enforcement."

"Hardly, but there was a time I walked the same street."

"On the other side, perhaps?"

"It's only a matter of time before someone gives something up. There's always someone besides the guy who did the crime who knows."

"The answer *who* is obvious."

"You know who? Tell me. I want to talk to them."

"It is Allah, of course. 'And not a leaf falls but He knows it.' "

"I'll have to take your word on that one, but I do know one thing. Someone's going to take a fall for killing Frankie Jr. and it sure as hell isn't going to be my friend Hark."

## 21

The San Francisco County Jail in San Bruno was shaped like a giant four-leaf clover, but anyone imprisoned there had run out of luck long before. The hulking complex wedged between San Andreas Lake and the Pacific Ocean stood atop the biggest earthquake fault in the state. A thick blanket of fog usually covered the jail and added to the bleakness of its concrete walls. The stench of mildew and faulty plumbing extended past the main gate.

Jack held his nose and emotions in check at the heavily guarded entrance. Cicero Broadshank had paved the way so he was able to pass through with minimal hassle and no body cavity search. The portly lawyer met him in the visitor's waiting room.

"What the hell happened?" Jack said.

"Apparently, circumstances unfolded that surpass even my considerable powers and resources. Mr. Martinez was involved in another altercation, this one more serious than the first. He was transported here at three this morning."

"Is he hurt?"

"I have not been provided with a full medical report, but I

believe it safe to assume he is ambulatory or they would have admitted him to the prison ward at San Francisco General Hospital."

"What went down?"

"I possess only meager details, my boy. It appears the door to Mr. Martinez's cell was unlocked under suspicious circumstances after lights out. A pair of unescorted inmates entered and an attack on his person transpired. A weapon was recovered by the guards. It has been described as a piece of sharpened metal taped to the handle of a hairbrush. Ownership has been disclaimed by all involved. It is now the subject of an internal investigation."

"No doubt it belonged to the guys who tried to shank Hark. Are they dead or alive?"

"You have considerable confidence in your friend's abilities to fend off two armed assailants."

"Hark was weaned on gang rumbles and did two tours in Afghanistan. If he's walking, that means the other two aren't."

"We would not be having this conversation nor be allowed to visit him if one or both of the assailants was deceased."

"So, what are we waiting for?"

"It would appear this gentleman." Broadshank motioned to a guard armed with a clipboard.

He checked their IDs and then led them into a room that featured a row of cramped stalls. Each faced a darkened window. Jack and Broadshank sat. A light switch was thrown on the other side of the thick glass and Hark shuffled into a narrow booth. The door closed behind him. He was handcuffed. Broadshank picked up a telephone handset and gestured for Hark to do the same. Jack leaned in close so he could listen.

"I am doing everything in my power to get to the bottom of this ghastly situation," the lawyer began. "I will be filing a grievance within the hour charging the San Francisco Sheriff's

Department with gross malfeasance for securing your cell improperly."

"All that will do is make it tough on the screws who'll make sure their fellow officers down here make it tough on me," Hark said.

"Who was it?" Jack said.

Hark was wearing his game face, but his eyebrows beetled. "Couple of tweakers from another block."

"Why?"

"That's what I asked them. At least the one who was still awake. He said they did it for a pack of smokes and a quarter of crank."

"Who put them up to it?"

"Said it was a contract came from the outside. Must be somebody who doesn't want to see me walk."

"Wonder Boy will find out."

The lawyer interrupted. "I must remind you these conversations are not private even though they are protected by attorney-client privilege."

Hark said to Jack, "How's Vinny doing?"

"He's still holding down the store as far as I know."

"You haven't been by?"

"You asked me not to pick at it so I'm not picking. I'm doing what they call *pursuing other options*."

Hark raised his chin. "Vinny's a good kid. He don't need any of my shit rubbing off. But that customer, the one with the design? You find out anything from Rosa?"

"Some."

"He a good customer or what?"

"It's complicated."

Hark leaned his forehead against the glass. "How she doing?"

"She's worried about you, but it's not like she hasn't been worried before."

Hark's lips tightened against his teeth. "This time's different. Keep an eye on her, okay?"

"Already doing it."

Hark turned to Broadshank. "Getting sent down here, what's that going do to my prelim date?"

"Nothing. State law is quite specific on the schedule. It will proceed as Judge Chun scheduled: ten court days after your arraignment. The time is drawing near. You and I shall have an opportunity to meet immediately prior to the hearing to discuss the procedure."

"I'll make sure to stay alive until then."

Broadshank made fish faces.

Jack said, "Did they put you in general population or a special unit?"

"GP," Hark said. "I'm bunking in a quad."

"CB will see about moving you into a single."

"Won't matter. I was in a single when they came after me."

Jack sucked his teeth and said to Broadshank, "Can't you force them to arrange extra security?"

Hark said, "What happened at the Hall already spread via the grapevine. Namely, who walked in and who got carried out. That's news I can use. It's all about respect down here. Nobody's going mess with me after hearing that."

"Unless they don't have a choice."

"You worried about me, *vato*? I'm touched."

"I'm worried about Rosa and what she'll do to me if something happens to you."

"Come after you with that big ol' ladle of hers like she used to when we were kids. Thing stung. Tell her they got me working in the kitchen."

"Good idea. She'll like that."

They grinned at each other like fools.

The door to the booth opened and a guard told Hark time was up.

When he stood, the grin disappeared. "Next time I see you *'mano*, let me know what you find out about that customer. I been thinking on it. That design rings a bell from a long, long time ago."

Hark's expression told Jack the memory was not a pleasant one.

## 22

I t was Sunday and JFK Drive through Golden Gate Park was closed to cars. Rollerbladers and families pushing prams took over the road as music drifted in the air along with the smell of barbecues. Players in pickup soccer games swarmed the meadows while lines formed at the entrances to Cal Academy of Sciences and the de Young Museum. An orchestra played ballroom music in the Bandshell. Old timers and hipsters waltzed to it.

Jack and his family followed the path to Stow Lake. Zita ran ahead as Katie pushed Harry in a three-wheeled jogging stroller.

"That thing reminds me of the auto-rickshaws we rode in Kathmandu," he said.

Katie laughed. "Tuk-tuks."

"That's what they call them in Thailand, but yeah, same thing. Remember when we took one to the Sundarijal Waterfall? We got off lucky. The road was steep and narrow and the driver flying on betel nut. He was crazy."

"So were we. Crazy in love. Now look at us. A chance encounter in a Himalayan teahouse and two kids later."

"Right time, right place, I suppose."

"Karma," she said.

"That and the glowing triangle position you insisted was surefire for pregnancy."

She leaned over and punched his shoulder. "Shush. The children."

They found a spot alongside the lake. Katie spread out a picnic blanket and Jack unloaded a backpack filled with cartons of food and a chilled bottle of Vermentino. A flotilla of brightly painted wooden row boats passed by.

"Let's go for a boat ride. Please?" Zita pleaded.

"I'll take you after we eat," Jack said. "You can row while I nap in the bow."

She plopped down on the checkered blanket. Katie filled plates while Jack poured the crisp Italian white wine.

"To many more Sunday's in the park," Katie said as she and Jack clinked plastic.

"Next time let's dress up like the folks in the painting by Georges Seurat."

"My husband the art aficionado," she said.

Jack grinned, but kept the truth to himself. His knowledge of masterpieces had been part of his training as a con artist. He'd spent his early years teaming with a master forger by the name of Henri Le Conte, Harry's namesake.

Katie and the baby napped after lunch while Jack and Zita strolled over to the boathouse and rented a bright red row boat. He fitted her into an orange life jacket and they sat side by side on the thwart.

"You hold the oars like this and pull toward you," he explained. "You want to go right, you push the left oar and pull the right. See?"

She gripped the handles and he placed his hands on either side of hers. In no time, they were circling Strawberry Hill. Sunbeams cast sparkles on the water. A great blue heron stalked fingerlings in the shallows. A pair of mallards trailed by six ducklings paddled by.

Zita said, "Is Uncle Hark going to be okay?"

"What makes you say that?" Jack said.

"I heard you and the policeman."

"That was grown-up stuff."

"I saw it on TV also."

"What did you see?"

"A lady said he was in jail. Did your friend catch him?"

Jack cursed Shauna Rhames under his breath. "I thought you weren't supposed to watch TV without Katie and me."

"I didn't."

"Then how did you see it?"

"A lady was watching TV on her bicycle at Katie's gym."

They rowed past the Golden Gate Pavilion, a red Chinese peace pagoda topped by a green tile roof.

"Wait a minute," Jack said. "Those screens only play sound through headphones. How did you know what the reporter was saying?"

"I read it. The TV had words."

"Closed caption," Jack said.

"Did Uncle Hark do something bad?"

"No, *mija*. The police made a mistake is all."

"Will he be at *Abuelita's* tomorrow?"

"Not tomorrow, but soon. I promise."

"Okay," she said. "*Promotiste*."

THEY PACKED up the picnic and were walking back through the park when the familiar chords of a rock song rang from the other side of a stand of redwoods. Jack led his family off the main path to have a look. A large crowd was gathered in front of a stage that had been erected in a meadow. People were swaying to the music with their hands raised. Some played air guitar, others danced in place as the lead singer did a fair cover of "City of Blinding Lights."

Zita started clapping her hands. Katie danced with Harry cradled in her arms.

When the music faded, the lead singer clutched the microphone. "Now please give it up for the man with a plan to save San Fran. I give you the next mayor of our great city, Supervisor Erick Berlin."

The applause was even louder than that for the band. Berlin ran onto the stage like a rock star, pumping his fist and high-fiving the singer. He acknowledged the crowd with a wave.

"Thank you, thank you. It's my honor to be here with you today in the city that invented rock and roll."

The line was a surefire hit and Berlin stood there grinning, absorbing the energy from the crowd as they let loose with an even more thunderous round of applause. After a couple of minutes, he motioned for quiet.

"I look out in this field and I see everything that's great about San Francisco. I see black, white, and brown faces. I see LGBT and straight. I see singles, I see families. I see the young and I see seniors. I'm reminded of what my grandma Ethie taught me. A community is a family. We are all related."

Cheers and whistles pieced the sky.

Berlin used his hands to quiet down the raucous crowd. "You know what else I see? I see this great big family of ours all wants and deserves the same things. Freedom. Respect. Safety. Security. If I'm so fortunate to become your mayor, I will work every second of every day to make sure no one goes wanting. And that starts with making sure no one goes hungry. No one goes without a roof over their head. No one lives in an unsafe building. And no one is threatened by crime. Folks, I promise you, that with your help, we can have all those things. Join me. Join me on election day and let's show the world what our San Francisco family can do. Thank you. Thank you."

On cue, the band struck up again as the audience mixed applause with cheers and then more arm waving and dancing as Berlin stood alongside the lead singer.

Jack scanned the stage and the crowd. He spotted Ricky Udo standing in the wings. Udo returned the stare and made his fingers into a gun and aimed it at him.

"Let's go," Jack said.

"You don't want to stay for another song?" Katie said.

"I've seen everything I need to."

## 23

Threstreetlights wore halos. A jet circling above the
midnight fog left a muffled whine in its wake. The
metal lid of a dumpster clanged as a garbage truck
hoisted it into the air and emptied the stinking waste into its
gaping maw.

Jack gave the front door to Hark's shop another knock. He
raised his chin to the camera lens fixed above the door so Vinny
Vargas could get a clear look.

The kid finally called from the other side of the locked door.
"That you, Jack..., uh, Mr. McCoul?"

"You called me. Who else would it be this time of night?"

The door creaked open. The hair on the back of Jack's neck
rose, and he instinctively eased onto the balls of his feet as he
kept his tone casual. "You said you needed to talk. What's up?"

"The dude from the other night came back," Vinny said.

"LOCO OCHO. He show his knuckles to the camera again?"

"Yeah. That and knocked on the door."

Jack could read the kid's face as easily as a phone display.
"He's in there with you."

"Uh-huh."

"He got a gun on you?"

"No. He says he only wants to talk. To you."

"About what?"

"About Geraldo Martinez," a voice graveled by cigarettes called from inside the darkened room.

"You mean Hark," Jack said.

"If that's his handle," the man said.

"What about him?"

"Come on in. I don't bite."

"Why not step out here?"

The man coughed. "I seen you round town plenty. If I wanted to hurt you, you'd already be hurt."

"Well, with an invitation like that, how can I refuse?"

The shop area was still cloaked in darkness, but a light shone in Hark's private office. The man stayed in the shadows as he walked toward it. Jack and Vinny followed.

When they were inside, the man said, "Shut the door."

Jack closed it behind him. The man pulled the chair around from Hark's desk and indicated with a tattooed finger for Jack and Vinny to sit on a couch that used to be the rear bench seat in a 1978 Dodge van.

Jack said, "Should I call you LOCO or Benicio?"

Tuxtla's lip curled, revealing nicotine stained teeth. A couple were missing. "You talked to that old *bruja*. She never liked me. Still blames me. She tell you that?"

"What do you want?"

Tuxtla looked down at his fists. His knuckles weren't the only thing blued. He was wearing a dark sweat shirt with the hood pushed back, but jailhouse ink showed at his neck and wrists. His scalp was buzzed but the stubble receded like the tide. His complexion was as gray as dawn.

"I got sent down for something had nothing to do with her daughter. Nothing at all. Still, she blames me. Folsom Prison?

That song makes it sound like a church camp, but it ain't." He put a tattooed fist to his mouth and coughed into it.

"What do you want with Hark?" Jack asked.

"I'm down there all these years I never heard from nobody. Not the *bruja's* daughter, not my own mother. But, okay, I never sent word back neither. Way it's got to be when you're in the twilight zone."

"That's what lifers call it. If you're one, how'd you get out? Tunnel like El Chapo?"

"You got some mouth on you, *güero*, you know that?"

"You're not the first to tell me that."

"What's with you, treating that old lady like she's your *abuelita*. You some kinda Mexican wannabe, hanging with the brown homies?"

"She *is* my *abuelita*. Hark and I are closer than blood. What do you want with him?"

Tuxtla sighed. "There was a time, *pendejo*, I woulda dragged you behind my whip disrespecting me like that."

Jack started to stand. "And there was a time I would've sat here and listened to your bullshit, but I've grown old myself. I need my beauty sleep. Vinny, make sure to take some 409 to that chair after *Señor* OCHO leaves."

Tuxtla coughed again. "Okay, *ese*. You're a tough guy. *Despacio*. How 'bout a hand, eh? I want to talk to Geraldo. Hark, you call him. Like the old lady told you, her daughter and me were tight once. I tried to get a line on her. But it's like she's one of *los desaparecidos*."

"Some might think you had something to do with that."

"*Chingate*."

Jack could feel Vinny squirming on the bench seat next to him.

"What makes you think Hark knows where his mother's at, gone all these years?"

Tuxtla shrugged. Bony shoulders poked the hoody like the ends of a hanger. "He's a line to her is all."

Jack leaned back. "You on some kind of apology tour?"

"¿*Que?* What's that supposed to mean?"

"It's what people do when they find Jesus or get a death sentence. Go around and say they're sorry. What's yours, Christ or cancer?"

Vinny squirmed again. "Oh man, that's cold, dude. Real cold."

Tuxtla waved the kid off. "Why doesn't matter. What does is I find her. I heard she moved to L.A. I went there. *Nada.*"

"You wasted your time. Some people go on vacation every year, Hark goes looking for his mother. If anybody could've found her, it'd be him."

"Why I'm back in San Francisco, but I guess I got here too late to ask him."

"You could visit him in jail."

Tuxtla shook his head. "Not a good idea."

Jack took in the man's face, his thin frame. He remembered his mother when she was toward the end. An empty dress. That's what he'd thought when chemo hadn't worked and the cancer had stripped away all the softness.

"You think you're Hark's father." Jack didn't form it in a question and he expected Tuxtla to launch himself across the room.

The convicted murderer only sighed. "I don't know. Maybe. What I wanted to ask his mother. I found out she was in a family way the day I got busted. In the joint, I told myself it coulda been some other *pachuco's.*"

"So, now what, hope springs eternal?"

"Oh, cold, dude. Cold," Vinny muttered.

Tuxtla's lips curled against a wall of bared brown teeth with black openings. "You got a kid?"

"Two." Jack knowingly broke his rule of never bringing up

his family to people in the life.

"Then you're set forever. Your rep will never die. They carry you on with 'em."

"Who needs kids?" Vinny crossed his arms. "Bunch of snot noses running around. I'm never going have 'em. My old man? I barely knew him and that's fine by me."

Jack and Tuxtla exchanged knowing glances. Jack said to Vinny, "You're lucky Hark took you in."

Tuxtla said, "Does he know about me?"

"I don't know. I showed him a picture of your fists when you showed them to the camera. Something about them might've rung a bell, but I can't be sure."

"Got my knucks inked when I was sixteen and joined the *vatos* who protected our block on Guerrero Street."

"*Los Guerreros*," Jack said, rolling the *r*'s. "*The soldiers.* Tough bunch."

"We was, but that was a long time ago. They put me away and my *hermanos*..." He blew air between his lips but it made no whistle. The effort made his face even grayer.

Jack said, "Hark was arrested on a bullshit charge. He's on the wrong end of some kind of political mashup that needed somebody convenient. I can get word down to him if you want."

"Down? I thought he was up on the seventh floor."

"That was then. This is now. Somebody took a run at him with a shiv. They sent him to San Bruno."

"He defended his honor? Good. He *macho*?"

"*Muy.*"

Pride flickered across Tuxtla's drawn face. "You got to be in this life. In any life."

"He's got a preliminary hearing coming up, but even then, they could keep him at San Bruno for a year or so before trial. Different jail, but same circumstances." Jack didn't have to cross the t's for a pro like Tuxtla.

The con nodded. "I'll ask around, see if somebody there don't owe me a favor. Make sure he gets all his meals and time in the yard. Someone to spot him while he's on the bench pumping iron."

"That'd be good."

Tuxtla said, "This *güero* he supposedly hit, who is he?"

"A rich man's pride and joy."

"Spoiled rotten, eh?"

"To the bone."

"Geraldo. Hark, I mean. They have history?"

"His father bought the building Hark's grandma's restaurant is in. They're jacking up the rent. The son came in and tried to throw his weight around. You can guess what Hark told him. The DA will use it as motive."

"Who's the dead kid's old man?"

"Frank Penny."

Benicio Tuxtla's cough made him bend at the waist. When he recovered, he said, "I remember him. He was small time when I was coming up. Owned a couple of buildings on Guerrero Street. Charged too much, fixed too little. Always calling the man on us for doing nothing more than perching on the stoop."

"Penny grew older and richer. More powerful too."

"Don't they all."

Jack studied him, trying to see if he could find anything in Tuxtla's face or mannerisms that were like Hark's.

Tuxtla stood. "I got to go."

"I hear something, how do I pass it on to you?"

"Tell the kid here. He can be the cutoff."

Vinny sat up straighter. "Yeah, man. Like, I can do that. *No problema.*"

Jack and Tuxtla both looked him and then at each other. Their expressions said the same thing: *there was always a problem.*

orning light streaming through the loft's bedroom window woke Jack. He reached over for Katie, but her side of the bed was empty. Laughter and clatter came from the kitchen. So did the beckoning scent of coffee. He threw on jeans and a T-shirt only to find Katie and the kids already dressed and heading for the door.

"What gives?" he said.

Katie mimed looking at a watch. "Well, look who's up, and it's only eleven."

Jack yawned. "That early?"

"Rough night?"

"Let's say it was enlightening. Where are you guys off to?"

"Harry and I are going to the Oakland gym. I'm interviewing new personal trainers. I'll drop Zita at her playdate on my way."

"Who with?" he asked Zita.

"LaTosha. She has a new puppy named Rasta. He looks like a mop."

"How do you know her?"

"From preschool. We have fun."

"I thought you didn't like preschool, said it was for babies."

"We're not babies, we're friends. Just like the policeman and you."

"What policeman?" Katie asked.

"Terry dropped by."

"You didn't tell me. What did he want?"

"Meet the kids. Pat them on the head."

"He did? What did he say about them?"

"Said Harry was as beautiful as you."

The baby farted and spit up at the same time. Mashed bananas and rice cereal trickled down his chins.

"I see what he means," Jack said.

"You're bad," Katie said.

"Not all the time."

"Only when it counts." She blew him a kiss. "Your night to cook dinner."

"Sure, what do you want?"

"Surprise us."

The loft turned quiet as the door closed behind them. Jack filled a mug and retreated to the couch. There was a time when he'd enjoy sitting alone with his thoughts, but now it felt like he was missing out on something. Since Katie and the kids came into his life, things were moving fast. Every day was new, and his old self was being pushed further and further into the past. There was no way to reclaim his life of fleecing fat cats and living large, but he also knew he could never let go of every part of it. What made him good at what he did also made him able to survive. Violence, evil, and danger weren't restricted to the underworld. They lurked a lot closer to the surface than most people wanted to believe.

Jack shook off the thought and turned his attention to his e-mail. One of the unreads had the subject line *Quid Pro Quo*. He didn't recognize the sender's address, but he knew it was from

Terry using an anonymous account to hand him something in exchange for sniffing around the Garza murder.

*Routine background check on V. Songprawati revealed lapsed B-2 visa. ICE flagged it.*

Someone overstaying a tourist visa never used to be a big deal, but with the one-eighty in the White House, new rules meant all bets were off. San Francisco defended its status as a sanctuary city, but even that future was in jeopardy. Jack punched in Valentine Song's phone number. All he got was voice mail.

"Valentine, it's Jack McCoul. I need to talk to you about something really important. Call me right away."

He gulped the coffee and got going. His first stop was the Gold Rush. The hostess in the flimsy teddy showing off safety pin jewelry said Valentine hadn't been to work for a couple of days.

"She called in with some excuse about studying for a test, but I think she's working extracurricular. Probably a conventioneer in town with a luxury suite and expense account. Or maybe she got real lucky and landed a local sugar daddy with an office downtown and a family in the suburbs."

"You're not exactly a-dues-paying member of Emily's List, are you?"

"Who's Emily?"

"Valentine comes in, tell her to call me. She has my number."

JACK RODE BART to Twenty-Fourth and Mission. The Double Dice was open for business and a few of the old timers were planted at the bar. DD Mitchell was sitting at a corner table thumbing through a stack of bills.

"Seen Valentine?" Jack asked.

DD looked up. "She only works evenings."

"How about last night?"

"What's it to you?"

"It's important. When was the last time you saw her?"

The sheave of papers fluttered to the table as DD let go. "Are you asking as her landlord or something more?"

"Easy, DD. You look a little green behind that lumberjack beard."

"Piss off."

"I already told Valentine I'm happy for her. Love makes the world go round. So, I'm going to ask again. Nicely. When was the last time you saw her?"

DD waved his hand. It made the tattooed dice tumble. "Easy, man. What's the big deal?"

"Freedom. Hers." He told him about the expired visa.

"Okay, okay. Let's see, couple days now. She's going to school out at City College. Computers and stuff. She has to put in extra time because it's all in English. Did you know she's only been speaking it a year?"

Jack gripped the back of a chair and leaned in. "When you hired her, did you ask to see her visa?"

"Why, are you going to rat me out to the border patrol? If you want to find someone to sell out, take a walk up and down Mission. It's a full menu out there."

"I'm asking because we're in the same boat here. I didn't check on her status when I became her landlord either. Student visa, tourist visa, green card, what do I care? Everybody's got to make a buck."

"Who told you hers was expired?"

"It came up when she discovered Garza's body. Now she's on ICE's screen."

The bartender maintained a stone face. "I hate to say it, but it's not my problem."

"Sure it is. You hired her."

"Do you know how many dishwashers I got coming through here every year? Servers? Most of the time I ask for paper they show me something you can buy online and print yourself. It's a joke. And the man in DC who wants to build a wall and send 'em back? Let him come wash my dishes, serve the drinks, because none of the techie kids around here are ever going to. Not on their six figure salaries and stock options."

"I need to let her know what's about to come down. There's a lawyer who might be able to straighten things out."

"Did you try her apartment?"

"When I called I got no answer. She hasn't been at the Gold Rush for a couple of days either. Come on, man. She needs our help."

DD pulled out his phone and clicked a speed dial. "Hey Val, it's me. Give a call."

He picked up the bills. "There. I did what I can."

"You're going to get pulled into this whether you like it or not."

"How's that?"

"Your turn to do the math. You run a bar. You're sleeping with your cocktail waitress. She's part of a murder investigation. She's got an expired visa. ICE must decide whether or not to deport her under the new rules. They start digging, what are they going to find? Surprise, surprise. She's tied to yet another murder. This one the son of your landlord who had a hard-on for her and wound up with his eggs scrambled outside your back door. A bar full of customers witnessed you and Frankie exchanging words. Half of them probably recorded it and uploaded it to YouTube. The other half surely tweeted about it.

The ICE guys aren't homicide cops, but they like to think they're in the same class."

"You watch too much TV."

"The only motive for murder older than money is jealousy."

"Who said anything about being jealous?"

"When ICE questions her, she's going to tell them Frankie was a douche and you're her knight in shining armor. The next door they'll knock on is yours."

DD pointed at him. "What are you going to tell them when they ask if you checked her paperwork?"

"I don't tell cops the time of day. Help me find her so I can put her in touch with Cicero Broadshank. He'll erect a legal wall around her better than anything Washington wants to build."

The bar owner finally nodded. "Okay, I'll ask the staff. Maybe somebody knows where she's at."

"It's a start."

## 25

A ghost bus nearly pasted Jack as he jaywalked Mission Street. None of the passengers being whisked to their jobs in Silicon Valley looked up from their devices when the driver blasted the horn. He took the stairs to the second floor two at a time. His knock on Valentine Song's door went unanswered so he used his master key. The apartment smelled of jasmine. The top of a dresser held a makeshift altar with a Buddha, candles, and wilted flowers. A colorful batik spread covered the bed. The closet was filled with clothes. A pair of empty wheelie suitcases were stored in the back.

Jack locked up and crossed the hall. He sent her a text and then found the number for City College. The receptionist treated him like a stalker and the phone died in his hand when he asked for Valentine's class schedule.

He was calculating his next move when someone knocked. It wasn't the Thai *émigré*, but it was a surprise. Wonder Boy had never visited his office before. Nor his home, either, for that matter.

"You s-s-seem preoccupied," the sibilant challenged bartender said.

"I got a tenant gone missing. ICE is targeting her over a lapsed visa. She's the one who found Garza and was also being hassled by Frankie Penny."

"The probability of being connected to a s-s-second murder is—"

"What I really need is her whereabouts."

"I will put the word out on the s-s-street."

"Thanks. What brought you here? Must be important."

Wonder Boy didn't drive or take public transportation even though he could recite BART and Muni routes and timetables at will. Flight schedules too.

"I have s-s-something for you, but I s-s-suggest you go to Action News' live s-s-stream first. S-S-Shauna Rhames is on with breaking news."

Jack didn't ask Wonder Boy how he knew that. He clicked the URL and pivoted the laptop so they could both watch. The reporter's carefully made-up face filled the screen.

"I'm here at city hall with an Action News exclusive. The board of supervisors has voted to pass emergency earthquake legislation." Rhames caught her breath as the camera pulled back to reveal Supervisor Berlin standing beside her inside the building's ornate gold and marble rotunda. "Joining me is Erick Berlin. Supervisor, can you explain to our viewers what this new law means."

"Certainly, Shauna. The Board approved an emergency ordinance to protect people living and working in seismically unsafe buildings. There are hundreds of such buildings throughout the city and thousands of families at risk. The new law takes effect immediately."

"Does this mean existing laws aren't up to the job?"

"The current seismic standards date back to the 1989 Loma Prieta earthquake, but seismic engineering practices have improved dramatically since then. So has our understanding of earthquakes. Not only are the standards out of date, but the process to retrofit buildings and inspect the work is taking too long. The new ordinance provides the City the ability to fast track state-of-the-art seismic upgrades and initiate redevelopment projects to provide safe housing and workplaces for families."

"I understand this emergency ordinance is your brainchild."

The camera zoomed in on Berlin. His shrug was meant to be self-effacing. "My grandma Ethie taught me you can get a lot done if you don't worry about who gets the credit. I'm honored to be in a position where I can help protect people. That is reward enough."

"The camera zoomed in on Rhames. "There you have it. San Franciscans are getting tougher seismic safety standards from a man who may have his sights on the mayor's office, but whose true ambition is serving the people. Reporting live from city hall, this is Shauna Rhames."

Jack killed the link as the stream cut to an ad for laxatives. "That was slick. Notice how Berlin slipped *redevelopment* in there. He gave the City a green light to red-tag buildings at will. I wonder how many won't meet the new standards and have to come down?"

"Thirty-s-s-six percent," Wonder Boy said.

"Cue the wrecking balls. Developers must be running out of champagne, toasting each other."

"S-s-some already have."

"Don't tell me you keep tabs on wine stocks in this town."

"S-s-several development companies took s-s-steps to position themselves to take advantage of this new s-s-standards months ago."

"Companies including Frank Penny & Son Real Estate?"

"Mr. Penny has expanded his business beyond s-s-selling real estate and managing rental properties."

"You got something, don't you?"

Wonder Boy extracted a white bar towel from his pocket and began polishing Jack's desk with the same care he gave to the historic plank at The Pier Inn. When he finished, he began folding the towel meticulously. He triangulated it and creased the corners with the same precision as a military honor guard readying an American flag to present to a fallen hero's family. When the bartender finished, he slipped the towel into his pocket.

"Don't make me beg," Jack said. "What is it?"

"Mr. Penny is a partner in a private capital group that has been investing in real estate throughout S-S-San Francisco. The group is called Better Tomorrow Capital. BTC for s-s-short. It has a s-s-special focus on providing capital to redevelopment projects."

"Including city-backed redevelopment projects?"

"Most redevelopment projects are public-private partnerships. They are funded by municipal bonds, s-s-state and federal grants, and private equity from entities like BTC."

"Any of Better Tomorrow's projects in the Mission?"

"Two s-s-small ones are underway and a very s-s-sizable mixed housing and retail project is at the planning s-s-stage."

"This new one, it's right here on Mission Street, isn't it?"

Wonder Boy placed a thumb drive on Jack's desk. "It holds s-s-several files, including a project description, architectural renderings, s-s-schematics, and blueprints. There is also a prospectus and financial s-s-statement from BTC."

"I can't believe that stuff is public."

"S-s-some of it is. Dodd-Frank regulates private equity firms. They are required to disclose financials, although the president is trying to s-s-stop that."

Jack whistled. "A secret project. How long have they had it in the works?"

"S-s-seven months, three weeks, and two days."

"They must have been waiting for Berlin's seismic law to spring it."

"S-s-several obstacles have s-s-stood in the way."

"Meaning property owners who don't want to sell. But now with the new ordinance, those buildings are going to be wearing a scarlet letter faster than Hester Prynne."

"Nathanial Hawthorne s-s-set his novel in a Puritan colony in Massachusetts, not S-S-San Francisco."

"I know, I know. The nuns made us read it at Saint Joe's."

Jack asked if the thumb drive could prove Better Tomorrow Capital was funding Erick Berlin's campaign, but Wonder Boy signaled no.

"Damn, that would have been too easy. I'm betting Berlin hatched this law to line his own pockets."

"I calculate the likelihood of proving that at 32 to 1."

Jack grinned. "That good, huh? You know I can't resist a long shot."

DAY TURNED into night and Jack kept at it, studying the materials on the thumb drive, reading Better Tomorrow Capital's financials. The site map of the redevelopment project was an overlay of Mission Street stretching three blocks on either side of Jack's building. Blueprints revealed one- and two-bedroom floor plans on the top floors, retail on the ground level. The street view rendering was a cheery depiction of people strolling along tree-lined sidewalks in front of modern-looking buildings with glass and blond-wood facades. All the people wore smiles and trendy clothes. The scene was the opposite of a Marvel comic book.

Jack reached into his desk drawer and pulled out a bottle of Jameson. He poured a couple of fingers into a relatively clean glass. "The Mission will become as homogenized as milk," he said to his laptop. "A couple of units will be earmarked for low income, but the rest will go for market rate."

Wonder Boy had been right about BTC's bare-bones financial statement. Coffee bar chalkboard menus listed more items. He scrolled through the group's prospectus. The descriptions of company history and mission were even lighter. The list of directors was dominated by entities whose names borrowed heavily from nature: Woodforest Capital, Cascade Partners LP, Firebrook Equity, Sierra Summit Investments. The names of partners and investors were printed in six-point type. Most were trusts and LLCs. He guessed the one called FP&S Properties was a spinoff of Frank Penny & Son Real Estate.

Berlin's earthquake safety ordinance was a lifeline thrown to the investors. Jack knew it as sure as he knew the rich and powerful treated cutting corners as their rightful due. He'd made plenty of big scores because of it. He Googled Erick Berlin's news clips and clicked on the supervisor's YouTube channel. He didn't have any popcorn so he substituted with whisky while he watched.

The videos dated back to Berlin's arrival on the scene as a community organizer. He exhibited all the skills learned in acting classes. Jack recognized them because he'd been a regular in the drama department when he attended SF State; the lessons came in handy for staging con games. Berlin could switch from enthusiasm to earnestness with a single change in expression. He peppered his speeches with personal anecdotes and homilies to earn his audience's trust and support. He often quoted something his grandma Ethie had taught him.

"She sounds too good to be true," Jack said to himself.

And with that he sat up. Overclaiming was one of the top trip-ups for a grifter. Jack's mentor had taught him to always seed a little doubt when making a pitch to a mark. It helped sell the scam because marks all shared a common trait: they thought they were smarter than anyone else and viewed another person's doubt as something they could take advantage of to earn an even larger payoff.

Jack Googled Berlin's personal history. His bio was short on details. His parents died young and he'd been raised by his grandmother. He described her as devout and commonsense. A profile that ran in the *Chronicle* quoted Berlin as saying his grandma Ethie made him promise on her deathbed that he'd always fight for the little guy.

Jack entered a search for Ethie Berlin. Lots of references to Berlin came up, but nothing for *Ethie* beyond a reference to a slang guide that referred to the word as a racist slur for people of ethnic origin. Jack figured it must be a nickname. He went to BabyNamesPedia and searched on girl names that started with *e t h*. It listed fifty-six. The majority were names he'd never heard of: Ethelberta, Ethelda, and Etheswytha. The only one he recognized was Ethel. He searched on Ethel Berlin. No hits. He rechecked the news clips. Berlin never mentioned whether Grandma Ethie was his paternal or maternal grandmother. Jack checked the supervisor's parent's names: Larsen D. and Catherine R. Berlin. No maiden name was listed.

"So are you Ethel B or Ethel R? Or are you one of the other variations?" he asked his laptop.

It didn't reply.

Hoping for inspiration, Jack kept hitting the backspace. The cache of searches flipped open like fanning the pages of a book. He stopped when he reached the last alphabetical entry on the BabyNamesPedia list. It was *Ethyl*.

"Who names their kid after a gasoline?" he wondered aloud.

And then something tugged at his memory. He'd seen the variation before. And recently. He reopened the files on the thumb drive and searched *Ethyl*. It was in Better Tomorrow

Capital's list of partners and investors: The Ethyl Rodgers Estate Trust.

Jack typed a new URL: *blackpearl.bf*. The anonymous Burkina Faso top-level domain was a notorious bazaar for illegal transactions and the BlackPearl site was the Silk Road for hackers. He submitted a request seeking information on The Ethyl Rodgers Estate Trust. Jack drummed his fingers while he waited for a hacker residing in some dark corner of the cyberworld to respond.

He didn't have to wait long. An e-mail alert triggered. He opened it. The sender said details of the trust could be bought for $500 USD.

*Sold*, Jack typed. He sent payment and ten minutes later received an e-mail containing two files.

The first contained a copy of the South Dakota registration document for The Ethyl Rodgers Estate Trust. South Dakota was a favored place for trusts since it was one of only seven states in the country that imposed no tax on accumulated trust income. The trust was administered by a bank in Sioux Falls. The second file was a copy of a recent statement hacked from the bank. It was for The Ethyl Rodgers Estate Trust's account. It listed three deposits totaling $2.7 million. The only debits listed on the statement was for a monthly trustee fee and a quarterly estimated federal income tax payment.

Jack toasted the screen with a shot of Jameson. "Condolences for your dear, departed granny, Supervisor Berlin. But it looks like your loss is also your gain. Capital gain, that is, don't you know?"

## 26

L ast call had come and gone. The bars on Mission Street were locked up tight and the Night Owl bus had made its last run. Jack was ready to head home too. All the hours studying the redevelopment project's plans and thinking of ways to leverage his discovery that Berlin was taking kickbacks had tied stones to his eyelids. He turned the computer off and walked downstairs. The sidewalk was empty and a van parked in front blocked his view of the street. He turned to make sure the front door had locked behind him when the van's doors flew open and footsteps pounded concrete. Jack wheeled around and came eye-to-eye with the black hole of a gun barrel.

"Surprise, motherfucker," Ricky Udo gloated. He was bookended by two sides of beef wearing black and silver team jackets that matched his.

"Well, if it isn't the Raiderettes," Jack said.

"Funny," the left one said.

"Not," his counterpart grunted.

Udo's eyes were jumpy and his blond goatee greasy. "Give me back my gun."

"Try looking in your hand," Jack said.

"Not this one, the Smith 9 you sucker punched me for."

"Spanked you with a sack of potatoes, you mean."

Left beef smirked. Right beef showed more tonsils.

"You're gonna pay for that," Udo said. "Grab him."

Left and right rushed Jack and pinned him against the front door. Udo smacked the gun across Jack's jaw. Teeth cracked. Blood sprayed.

The two beefs grunted. "Yeah."

Jack kept his feet. He swallowed instead of spit. If his teeth were knocked out, at least he'd know where to find them.

Udo slammed the gun butt into his stomach. "How do you like that?"

The pair prevented Jack from doubling over. Udo hit him under the chin with an uppercut to lift his head and then raked the gun barrel across his temple.

"Welcome to fight club, motherfucker," he crowed.

He slipped the gun into his pocket and began pummeling Jack's midsection like it was a heavyweight bag, chanting, "A left and then a right, left and then a right."

Bright lights exploded. Echoes filled his ears. Jack slumped but the thick-necked flunkies wouldn't let him fall. Fuzzy faces started to flash on and off with each punch. Katie and then Zita and then Harry. They flickered by so fast he couldn't grab hold of them. Hark, *Abuelita*, and Wonder Boy zipped past too in a fractured slide show that kept time with Udo's punches. The sidewalk beneath his feet turned into a bowl of Jell-O.

Jack sensed movement in the darkness behind Udo. "What is the meaning of this?" a voice asked.

"None of your fucking business unless you want some of the same," Udo said without bothering to turn around. He resumed his chant. "A left and then a right. A left. A left. And a right."

"Everyone is everyone's business," the voice said, the tone matter-of-fact. "You will let him go now."

"Beat it or eat it, raghead," one of the beefs snarled.

"Alas, that is not my destiny."

Jack squinted through a veil of blood streaming from his brow. He could make out Udo's face, and then a hand with a bent finger darted in from the darkness, grabbed the punk's fist in mid punch, and spun him around. Jack heard a smack followed by a sharp cry.

"Ow, motherfucker."

The beefs let go and Jack plunged to the sidewalk as if his strings had been cut. He landed in a sitting position, his back against the door. The pair rushed forward only to meet a blur of flying fists and feet. Grunts and curses and shrieks of pain shattered the night.

Jack kicked from where he sat in hopes of tripping one of the Raiderettes. The sidewalk concussed as if a tree toppled. He flailed his arms, but if he connected with anyone, he couldn't tell. He was losing all feeling. The Jell-O had reached his chin. His head started to loll. He heard another sharp cry.

"He's got my gun!"

And then three flashes preceded three bangs like lightning does thunder.

The Jell-O enveloped him completely and so Jack closed his eyes and stopped trying to tread.

THE ECHOES of the gunshots rolled on, but the ground beneath him was no longer concrete, and the head that lolled was not his, but that of a woman he once loved cradled in his arms. The flickering lights were no longer the sparks of nerve endings short-circuited by fists, but the life going out in her no longer sparkling blue eyes.

"Stay with me. Stay with me," someone said.

But she did not answer. Nor could he.

A hand reached out from the darkness not to strike him, but to touch his shoulder.

"She's gone, 'mano. She's gone."

"Hark? Is that you? I... I should've seen it coming. I could've stopped it. I could've saved her."

"You know there ain't no reverse gear in life."

"I could've saved her."

"Leave it. We got to get out of here."

"Where we going?"

Jack felt himself pulled to his feet, an arm reached around him. Another voice spoke.

"Please, my friend, you are to walk now. We must get you to hospital. I will assist you."

And so, Jack tried. One foot in front of the other, half stumbling, half being dragged. Everything was so mixed up. People. Place. Time. Voices. The dirt road that lead from where he'd been unable to keep Zita's mother from dying turned back into a sidewalk, but after a while it turned into a wheat field. A farmhouse stood in the distance. Jagged mountains rose behind it, their snowcapped peaks etched against a dusking sky.

"I couldn't save Grace, but I can save her child. Our child. My daughter."

"I understand completely. It was the same for me. Saving children is our sacred duty," a voice said.

"She's in that farmhouse. They're holding her because what her mother did."

"Perhaps you should not speak now to save your strength. We still have a distance to travel."

Jack kept walking, sometimes faltering, sometimes halting. Only the arm under his was firm and kept him from falling.

"She won't know who I am. Grace never told her about me."

"Time enough to explain afterward, *ese*. We got to get her out of there first."

"Hark, is that you? Where did you go?"

"You know I always got your back."

"She'll ask about her mother, and I'll have to tell her. She'll blame me."

"Only if you blame yourself."

"I could've done something. I know it."

"The only one to blame is the dead who bring it on their own self."

"How can you so be sure about that?"

"Alas, when death occupies your neighborhood, my friend, you know it to be true."

"Who is that? You're not Hark."

"A name is only as important as what one does to honor he who bestowed it."

"What neighborhood? The sandbox? That's what you always called the 'Stan. Hark, you listening?"

"Alas, there are many names to describe that part of the world. The Levant. Holy Land. A tragedy. A home."

"You're not Hark. Where are we?"

"Please, we are to hurry. You have lost much blood. I will carry you now, but I must warn you, it will cause you much pain."

Jack felt himself being draped over something. Hands locked around his wrists. There was a yank and his feet left the ground. He was sure his spine would snap. Then his cheek was next to someone else's. Labored breathing mixed with his own. He was in a fireman's carry. His father had demonstrated it plenty of times when he acted out a rescue from a burning building.

"Stop. Put me down. I got to get to my daughter. She's in danger. She's in the farmhouse up ahead."

"Roger that, *vato*."

"Hark, you're here."

"Where else would I be?"

"We don't know how many guns are in there."

"Would it matter if we did?"

"I suppose not."

"Suppose? *'Mano, 'mano*, you always been sure. Sure is who you are."

"But everything's different now."

"You know the thing about different? Give it time, it becomes the same."

"Even being a father?"

"We don't go in there and save your little girl, you won't be one. *¿Sabes?*"

"Maybe they already split."

"We both know there's no room for maybe in this world. We go in like we planned. And nobody's going be chasing us afterward. Like we planned. Okay?"

"I can see the building up ahead. The lights are on. They're awfully bright. Too bright. They'll see us coming."

"Remember the plan."

"You take the front, I slip in the back. I tell her that her mother sent me. To keep her eyes closed until it's safe so she won't see anything she'll have to learn how to forget."

"Lock and load, *vato*. It's go time."

The lights were bright. Voices were calling. A siren was screaming. Jack took one more step and was swallowed by darkness.

## 27

W arm waves washed over and through him. There was no pain, no worries, no regrets. The little girl was calling his name and holding his hand. That was all he needed.

Jack drifted. Cumulus clouds floated between blue skies and blue waters. He watched them from a window seat, his daughter sitting beside him, and Hark commanding the aisle with his bulky frame spilling out of the seat and a guard dog look set in his eyes, stopping even the flight attendants from asking questions.

"We're almost to San Francisco," Jack said.

"How do you know that?" Zita asked.

"Because I recognize the clouds."

"How?"

"They line up to enter the Golden Gate."

"What's the Golden Gate?"

"The front door to home."

The plane banked and the engines droned. And he floated. One day he would take her to where her mother's ashes were scattered, but there was no reason to think about that day now.

There was no reason to think about the days that preceded the flight from Argentina either. All there was to do was to listen to his daughter's voice, feel her hand in his, and float. Float on the soft clouds bearing him home.

Then Katie called his name. She was waiting at the end of a long, dark tunnel. He hurried toward her. When he drew close her face lit up when she saw the little girl running alongside him. He felt his own face flush when he saw the newborn clutched in Katie's arms. Everyone started talking all at once. Zita chatting away, Harry burbling, Katie asking questions. Lots of questions. Jack strained to make out the words. Someone was answering her, but he didn't recognize the voice.

"Hey," Jack said. But no one responded. "Hey," he said louder. Still, no response. His ears started to ring. "Hey!" he yelled. "Hey, I'm right here. It's me. Hey!"

Banging beeps replaced the ringing. The warm tide ebbed. Tingling turned into sharp jabs. Something was keeping his eyes from opening. He tried to bat it away, but his hands wouldn't respond.

"Hey!" He yelled it again.

"Easy now."

"What?"

"Easy now. Can you hear me? Mr. McCoul. Can you hear me?"

Jack tried to nod, but doing so unleashed a wild pack of black spots and red flames that made him cringe.

"Try not to move. I'm a doctor. You've been injured."

Jack tried to rip off whatever was covering his eyes, but his wrists seemed manacled. He kicked.

"Don't, babe. Listen to the doctor. Let him do his job."

"Katie?"

"I'm right here. Zita and Harry too."

"My eyes."

"We taped gauze over them as a precaution while you were unconscious. I'm going to remove it now," the doctor said. "You might feel a tiny pinch... and there you go."

Lights blazed. Jack blinked rapidly. He tried to rub his eyes, but his hands would not do what he wanted. The beeping became more rapid. The ceiling spun. Faces too.

"You've suffered a concussion," the doctor said. "It's important you lie still."

Katie's face came into focus. It was drawn and wan. "Oh, babe," she said.

He locked onto her eyes and held them steady. It slowed the room from spinning. "What happened?"

"You were mugged, but you're safe now."

"Where... where am I?"

"SF General."

The doctor leaned in again. "I'm going to shine a light. Without moving your head, try to follow it."

Jack's eyeballs ached tracking the beam as it moved up, down, left, and right.

The doctor snapped off his penlight. He spoke to Katie. "We'll keep him another night and reassess in the morning, but the fact he's awake now and can follow the light is a good sign." He gave Jack a parting glance. "Welcome back."

A nurse took his place. She adjusted the IV, checked the heart monitor, and unfastened the soft restraints strapped to Jack's wrists.

"We had to use these because you were trying to pull out your central line when they moved you up from the ER," she said.

"How long ago was that?"

"Two days."

Jack looked over at Katie. "Did I miss Hark's prelim?"

"No," she said. "Don't worry about that now." And she blew him a kiss. Zita imitated her.

"You're lucky," the nurse said.

He managed a grin even though it hurt. "My middle name, don't you know?"

JACK WOKE UP. Katie and the kids were gone. The ceiling light was off and the window dark with night. He reached for a paper cup of water on the overbed table. As he drank, he realized he wasn't alone.

"You look like hell," Terry Dolan said. He was sitting in a visitor's chair illuminated by the screen of the heart monitor.

"The bus that ran over me must've backed up for good measure."

"The nurse said they have a special name for patients as bruised as you. Eggplant."

Jack counted teeth with his tongue. He tasted three temporary caps.

"The stitched-up gash in your temple is the kind made by a pistol whipping. I've seen it plenty of times."

"You should change professions."

"The ER doctor told me he wasn't going to revive you if you coded. He saw the same sort of head trauma from IEDs when he served in Iraq."

"Go ahead and ask what you came to ask."

"Who did it?"

"Like the ER doc said, I was blown up. I don't remember a thing."

"That's convenient. What about the guy who brought you here? Maybe he knows? Who was it?"

Jack shrugged. He wished he hadn't. It unleased the wild pack of black and red again. "What did they say in the ER?"

"They call it the knife and gun club for good reason. Nobody has time to talk to anybody who isn't bleeding." Terry leaned forward. "A paramedic who was cleaning out his truck told me he saw you ride in on someone's back. Your horse unloaded you onto an empty gurney, called for help, and disappeared. I watched a replay from the security camera, but couldn't make out a face. A man goes out of his way to try and save someone's life and doesn't stick around to see if he succeeded, that doesn't strike you as odd?"

"Maybe I was just outside the front door when he picked me up."

"He carried you nearly a mile."

"How do you figure?"

"That's how far the hospital is from Mission Street."

"Who says I was there?"

"Because the Mission Station got a call about shots fired in your neighborhood. They sent a patrol car to investigate."

Jack took his time sipping from the paper cup. "What did they find?"

"A lot of blood in the doorway to your building."

"The doctor didn't say anything about a GSW."

"You weren't shot, but a black van parked out front sure was. Two tires drilled clean. A third round through the gas tank. It takes a pro to do that."

"Sounds like a drive-by."

"The flat tires and gas tank were curbside."

"What did the van's owner say?"

"He reported it stolen hours before."

Jack sipped more water.

Terry said, "Who worked you over and why?"

"I must have temporary amnesia."

"Did it have to do with the Garza murder?"

"Katie said I was mugged."

"You still have your wallet. Your phone too."

"I must've put up a fight for that phone. My kids' pictures are on it. You know how the ad goes: Priceless."

"Help me out here. I'm trying to solve a murder and now an attempted on you. What did you find out?"

Jack thought about handing over Ricky Udo, but not yet. Udo wanted his gun back for a reason. Jack knew leverage when he saw it. He had the gun stashed in his office safe.

"My memory comes back, I'll let you know," he said.

Terry sighed.

Jack said, "Now you sound like you got worked over."

"Everything used to be so simple before all this new money rolled into town. Husband catches his wife in bed with the neighbor and shoots them both. Case solved. A bank robbery goes south. Game over. Gangbanger takes out a rival. Easy as pie. But this time? Something's off and it all has to do with money and politics."

"It usually does," Jack said.

"When I was growing up the rules were simple. You obeyed your parents, ate fish on Friday and went to mass on Sunday. You did what the nuns told you. My father always said, 'You're Irish American, son, the police department will always be your family. Join the force and walk the walk and one day you could be captain. Who knows, maybe even chief.' So that's what I did, but look what's it's gotten me?"

"A nice suit and a lieutenant's salary. You're on your way."

"What about a real family? A wife and children, a house with a yard out in The Avenues. That was also my goal and look how it turned out?" His frustration was more grumble than whine. "You're the crook and you got it all. I'm the cop and I'm about to lose my shield."

"A hospital room's no confessional, Terry. Try Saint Joe's."

"All I want is to do my job without the brass interfering. If you know something about Garza's killing, tell me. I'll take a look at Frank Penny Jr.'s murder in turn. You got my word on it."

"Another *quid pro quo*, huh?"

"Yes."

"Okay, but remember this one from Latin class? *Auribus teneo lupum.*"

"I don't recall it."

"We could be holding a wolf by the ears."

"I thought you liked taking risks."

"I do, but I also don't like getting bit."

## 28

J ack left the hospital with a pocket full of pain pills and a nurse's warning that he was a damn fool echoing in his ears. The driver who picked him up asked if he was going to a costume party. Jack's hope that Katie and the kids would be out doing errands paid off when he got home. He knew what she'd say about his self-administered discharge.

The reflection of his upper torso in the bathroom mirror had him humming an old Deep Purple tune. The sutures in his temple rode above a shiner. His upper lip resembled a prune. He struggled into blood-free clothes. It only took five minutes to tie his shoes.

Jack was sitting on the edge of the bed trying to regain his equilibrium when the phone rang. The number was unrecognizable, but he answered anyway.

"Speak."

"Hey, *vato*," Hark said.

"You out? Caller ID wasn't Pay Tel."

"I wish. Dude gave me a burner. All of a sudden I'm everyone's best friend. What I'm calling about."

"You want me to be your best man at a jailhouse wedding? I'd be honored. Who's the lucky guy?"

"Remind me to laugh. The way it went down was four, five homies approached me in the yard. More jailhouse ink on their heads than pruno swilled on a Saturday night. Lots of *14* and *N* and sombrero over a machete tats."

"*Nuestra Familia* signs," Jack said.

"Roger that. I'm thinking, okay, they don't look like they're the recruiting committee, but I'm going put down as many as I can before they stomp me. Only, it's not that way at all. Dudes are all hey *ese* this, and *ese* that, and we be your *hermanos*. They slip me the burner, a couple packs of smokes, and a bag of crank."

"All this because of what happened on the seventh floor?"

"They say an old chieftain sent word to give me protection and so that's what they're doing, they being all about loyalty. You don't say no and stay alive in their world."

"Our Family still being the number one Latino gang in NorCal prisons."

"Well, *La Eme* may disagree, but, hey, I didn't exactly mention their rivals to them."

Jack played it cool, but he knew what was coming next.

"So, what I want to know is, who's this guardian angel took an interest in me?"

"And you think I know."

"I know you know."

"It's the guy with the tattooed knuckles who showed up at your place."

"That's what I figured. I told you seeing that ink tugged a memory string. Who is he?"

"His name is Benicio Tuxtla. He did time in Folsom. A lot of time. He's out now and looking to make amends."

"And how is it I'm one of those *amends*."

Jack sucked his teeth. He could feel cold through the temporary caps. His jaw was so sore it would be a long time before he brushed any kind of tooth. Shaving was out of the question for the foreseeable future.

"He dated your mother. He got sent down for killing a gang rival. Your mom was pregnant at the time."

"With me." Hark said it without delay. Getting it out there so it wouldn't fester.

"Tuxtla denied he was the responsible party and your *abuelita* says no way he was."

"She'll go to her grave before ever saying so."

"About the size of it."

"What do you think, I look like him?"

Jack thought before answering. "Tuxtla looks like... Well, it doesn't take a medical degree to see he's got cancer. Probably why they let him out early. He's doing a forgiveness tour with the little time he's got left. He came to your place hoping you could give him a bead on your mother. It's her he's looking for. I don't think he's owned up to being your dad, but I told him where you were. He said he'd get the word out you warranted respect."

"More like he's on a shakedown trip. Don't give him nothing. Don't let him get near my *abuelita*. Got it?"

"Understood."

"I got to go."

"I'll see you at the prelim."

But Jack said it to a dead connection.

It was a week of wonders. Wonder Boy wonders, that was. First, he'd come to Jack's office. Now he was at his loft.

"You s-s-should s-s-still be in the hospital," the savant said.

"You could s-s-suffer s-s-serious complications if you do not treat the condition."

"Plenty of rest and lots of downtime. So they told me. I'll follow doctor's orders when I have the time."

"Ice to the back of your neck will help. If you do not own an ice bag, a bag of frozen peas will s-s-suffice. They conform to the s-s-specific body part when applied."

"The only ice I want is in a glass of Jameson."

"Alcohol consumption is contraindicated with a s-s-severe concussion diagnosis."

"Maybe, but I bet it could help quiet down a couple of cracked ribs, three busted teeth, and a solar plexus that got pounded like a drum?"

"I s-s-see your point. S-s-should I mix you a libation?"

"Never mind. I got enough painkillers on board I could walk on glass and not know it. Did you bring me what I asked for?"

Wonder Boy nodded. He reached into his pocket and extracted a plastic sandwich bag containing a cell phone. "It is prepaid and better than the apps for s-s-smartphones that provide temporary numbers. This one can't be traced back like those."

Jack stuck the bagged burner into his own pocket. "What about Valentine Song? Were you able to get a bead on her?"

"S-s-she is s-s-staying with a fellow co-ed in a flat on Faxon Street right off Ocean Avenue. It is s-s-suitably close to City College campus."

"Valentine's apartment is only two BART stops away as it is, so there's got to be another reason she's bunking there."

"I was only able to determine her location, not her motivation."

"Thanks. I'll take a run out and see what's what."

"Driving is unwise when you have brain injury s-s-symptoms. The risk of aggravating a concussion is better than s-s-six to one."

"Now you're a neurologist in addition to a mixologist?"

"Both s-s-specialize in treating the head."

"Then maybe you can do something about this jukebox playing in mine."

Wonder blinked a few times. "The Pier used to have a S-S-Seeburg Disco 160. The number refers to the number of records it held. S-s-selection A1 was the Beatles "Hard Day's Night." A2 was—"

Jack cut him off with a limp wave of the hand. "You know what I really want to know? Anything about Frankie Penny that we can use to help free Hark. Frankie thought he was entitled to harass Valentine with no blowback. There's got to be something else out there. Spoiled punks leave a trail shinier than a snail's."

"I will ask around. Are you s-s-sure you do not want to hear the entire S-S-Seeburg catalogue?"

OCEAN AVENUE CUT A COOL, gray corridor through the southern part of the city. Fog was often slow to lift in the valley that lay between Mount Davidson and Excelsior Heights. Banks, Chinese restaurants, and liquor stores faced the avenue while tidy stucco homes and flats lined the cross streets.

Jack boarded the K Ingleside at Embarcadero Station. His head throbbed every time the rail cars jostled through a turn and bounced over seams in the track. His ribs ached so bad he had to stop and catch his breath before walking up Faxon. The address Wonder Boy gave him was a two-bedroom flat sandwiched between a street-level garage and top floor unit. A slim woman wearing a City College sweat shirt and a phone tucked beneath her chin answered the door. She seemed more annoyed for having to interrupt her call than alarmed by Jack's bandaged forehead and black eye.

"Val, you got a visitor," she yelled as she turned and walked away.

Jack followed her inside. The place smelled of cat box and overcooked ramen. A leaning tower of pizza boxes stood in the middle of a dining room table that hadn't seen wax for years.

Valentine appeared from a darkened hallway. "Oh hi, Jack. What you doing here? How you know where I am?"

"A little bird told me."

She gasped when he stepped into the light. "What happen? You have car wreck?"

"Something like that. How are you doing?"

"I am fine. I been staying here for couple days. We studying for big test. Very important this big test, okay?"

"Could I have some water? I'm taking medication that makes me thirsty."

"Oh yes, okay. You look like you going fall down. You better sit on couch. I bring you water. You want something to eat?"

"I'm good. Just the water."

He scanned the room while she busied herself in the kitchen. The furniture was Craigslist. The carpet in need of replacing or, at the very least, a good scouring with a Rug Doctor.

Valentine came back with a glass of ice water. Jack fished out a couple of cubes and pressed them against the back of his neck while he drank.

"Can you take a break from studying so we can talk?" he asked her.

She hesitated. "Okay, but only little bit. You the best, Jack, but big exam very important."

"So you said." He patted the couch next to him. The arms begged for a cat scratch post. "Your friend seems nice."

"Oh, yes. Cammy the best. She studying to be mortician."

"Good job security. Nice of her to let you stay here."

"Her roommate move out so I using room."

"You haven't been to your place for a while. Does this mean you're going to move here permanently?"

Valentine hesitated again. She started realigning the purple streak in her hair. "I like my apartment very much. You the best. Is it problem I not sleeping there? My rent all paid, yes?"

"That's not the problem."

"There is problem?"

"It's about your visa. Yours is no longer valid. The authorities have your name on a list."

Her eyes widened. "Oh, no. I not want get exported. That how you say it?"

"Close enough. I might be able to get you some help."

"What kind of help?"

"You need to talk to a lawyer. I have a friend who can steer you in the right direction. His name is Cicero Broadshank. He's got folks in his office who specialize in this sort of thing. I'll text you his contact info and let him know you're going to call."

"Lawyer cost lot of money. I cannot pay. I sending all extra money home to my mother."

"Don't worry about it. Just talk to him. If there's any fee I'll cover it."

"You pay? Why you do that for me?"

"You know the saying, you scratch my back, I'll scratch yours?"

Valentine dipped her head and giggled. "You never ask me that before. I always wonder how come. You the best, Jack. You want me to do special dance for you? I can dress as Rati and dance to Beyoncé. Very sexy. I do for you, okay?"

"No, I meant something else."

"Oh yes, but I not that kind of girl."

"Not that either. I need some information and I need you to be truthful. Can you do that?"

"I not lie to you."

"I need to know what happened the night Frank Penny Jr. died. All of it, everything you know and everything you saw. Don't leave out the parts you think are protecting someone."

"I already told you. I home and look out window and see Mr. Penny leave Double Dice. He talk to men and they all walk away. I not see anything more. That all I know. I promise. You believe me, okay?"

"Tell me about DD and Frankie."

Her hand went to her hair. "What about DD?"

"He argued with Frankie the night I was at the Double Dice. After I left. DD told him to keep his hands off you, didn't he?"

"I not sure."

"Yes, you are. Is that the reason you haven't been home? Did DD say something to you? Did he do something to scare you?"

"DD like me. I like him."

"Then how come you're staying here and haven't been to work at the Double Dice?"

Valentine looked down at her feet. "Girl take her clothes off for work, guy gets wrong idea about her. Sometime it better to play hard to get."

"Tell me about DD and Frankie."

"Okay, it nothing. No big deal. DD got mad. Mr. Penny drink too much and start talking about me. He say not nice things about way I look when I dance. How he likes my ta-tas and want go boom boom."

"He ever come and watch you dance at the Gold Rush?"

"Oh yes. Many times. He big customer there."

"By that you mean he left big tips?"

"Oh yes, no, I mean he come in a lot. He not always big

tipper. All the girls say he very cheap. Then one day he tip me a lot. Every dance he give me twenty, fifty, hundred dollar bill."

"Why the sudden change of heart? You do a special dance that day?"

"No, nothing special. I think he knew I was sad that day."

"How come?"

"It the day I go to work after finding Mr. Garza. I very sad. I like Mr. Garza. He the best."

"So, Frankie tried to cheer you up."

"I guess."

Jack did some calendaring. "It wasn't that long afterward he was grabbing at you at the Double Dice. The night I was there. He didn't seem too worried about your feelings then."

"He drink too much. He tried to reach under my dress and put money in my panties. Like I at Gold Rush wearing G-string. That only for when I am dancing, not serving cocktails."

"After I left, did DD and Frankie get into a fight?

"They say mean things to each other. DD grab Mr. Penny arm. Then Ricky Udo came in and tell DD not to touch him. DD laughed in his face. Ricky and Mr. Penny both left."

"So, DD and Frankie argued. Ricky Udo came in and broke it up. They leave. But DD doesn't eight-six Frankie. Frankie comes back to the Double Dice again. The night he was killed he was at the bar, but you were home studying. Frankie has a drink, sees you're not there and leaves. You look out your window and see two guys get out of a car and talk to him. They all walk away and you don't know what happened."

"Yes. That all true."

"Can you describe the two men?"

"Oh, yes, I could not see them so good."

"Big, small, short, tall?"

"Big. You know, sporting."

"How's that?"

"The kind watch sporting games on TV all the time. Go to stadium. Wear team clothes."

"Shirts and hats. How about jackets? These guys wearing team jackets?"

"Oh, yes, I think you right. They wore same jacket."

"What about Ricky Udo?"

"What about him?"

"He's usually with Frankie. Did you see him that night too?"

"Oh, yes. He leave Double Dice when Mr. Penny talking to two men."

"Did he go with them when they walked down the street?"

"I not know. I stop looking. I study school work and go to sleep. I not know Mr. Penny was getting killed. Am I in trouble?"

"As long as you're telling the truth, no."

"But my visa, I am in trouble for it?

"That's why you need to call my lawyer friend."

"Okay, I promise. You the best, Jack. You want me to scratch your back again, let me know. I can dress like Rati while I am scratching, you want."

"Thanks, but the only thing that itches right now are my stitches."

## 29

B eep's boasted a vintage neon sign with a blinking rocket ship and the best burgers in San Francisco. The joint was only six blocks from Faxon, but the walk left Jack gasping. The layers of tape around his chest made him think of pythons. He intended to order a vanilla shake, figuring he could at least get some nutrition through a straw, but the smell of Angus beef patties sizzling on the grill proved irresistible.

Most diners ate in their cars or ferried their orders home, but a handful of stools were set up along an outdoor counter. Jack straddled one at the end. His eyes, even the blackened one, turned out to be bigger than his punched-up stomach. He chalked his lack of appetite up to the pain meds, but the shake went down easy and he found he could nibble a fry without screaming out loud.

He mulled over the conversation with Valentine Song. It confirmed what his gut had been telling him since Ricky Udo worked him over. The Raiderettes were the men in the parked car outside the Double Dice. What happened after they shepherded Frankie into the dark alley wasn't rocket science. Udo showed up. Did he mean to mete out a spanking like a babysitter fed up with an unruly child and it got out of hand, or was Udo cleaning up a mess? If so, was it his mess or someone else's? The fact that the cops were quick to locate a suspect and then the DA promptly killed any further investigation suggested someone was pulling the strings. Someone with a whole lot of clout.

Jack tore off a corner of the burger and tried chewing on the side of his mouth where all the teeth were his own. It wasn't the onions that made his eyes water. He sucked some more milk-shake and wondered if he'd ever be able to enjoy a steak again. If not, he'd at least make Katie happy. She was quick to remind him that eating lower on the food chain was healthier for his heart, not to mention the planet. Whenever he countered that if it weren't for meat, humans would never have developed bigger brains, she'd volley right back: "It may have helped us evolve from Australopithecus to Neanderthal, but some of us have continued to progress. How about you, caveman?"

Normally thinking about their give and take and their bedroom remedy for soothing hot tempers and hurt feelings put a giddyup in his step, but now all he could think was how good it'd feel to put his feet up while wearing an ice bag. The K Ingle-side was clacketing down the tracks and Jack was sorely tempted to hop on board and go home, but knowing Hark's preliminary hearing was approaching faster than the light-rail cars squelched the thought. Udo and his pair of knuckle draggers deserved punishment, and the idea of personally sending them back to the Stone Age salved all wounds.

SAMI ALFASSI WAS FRESHENING the shelves. He wielded a feath-ered duster and chamois shoe shine rag simultaneously.

Jack said, "You're very adept with your hands."

Alfassi turned. His eyes were hooded, his demeanor calm. "A

man should respect any task he undertakes because the opportunity to work is a gift from Allah."

"I came to thank you for the other night. If it hadn't been for you—"

"It is not me you need to thank. I was only His instrument."

"Yeah, well, a pretty finely tuned one at that. Why do I think you were doing more than writing on chalkboards and grading papers back in Aleppo?"

"One does what one must to survive in a world where barbarism has become rule."

"I couldn't agree more. Look, I want you to know I owe you one. Whatever you need, whenever you need it, I'm good for it."

Alfassi gave the slightest of bows. Jack couldn't help but notice he didn't have a scratch on him. "There is no need to reciprocate, but I honor your sincerity and generosity."

"I'm glad you came along when you did, and you don't seem too much the worse for wear for it." Jack gestured at his own wounds. "Those dudes were throwing some mean punches."

"Praise be that I chose to stay late to check inventory. I fell asleep and when I awoke, I realized I had missed evening prayers. I was about to begin when I heard the noise."

"You're a brave man to wade in like that and take a gun away from a hood. Even as I was blacking out I could see you're no stranger to hand-to-hand combat. Not afraid of it either."

Again with a shrug, the shopkeeper said, "Anyone can be taught how to use one's fists and discharge a weapon accurately. The harder lesson is to learn when not to."

"Mind if I ask you a question?"

"If I can answer it, I will."

"What happened after you shot the van? I was taking a nap by then."

"These men are the ones who have been terrorizing the shopkeepers. They proved to be what most men are when they choose to victimize someone. Cowards. When I took the pistol away from Udo, his will to fight disappeared with it. I displayed my acquaintance with weaponry to encourage them to flee."

"Which they did at full speed. What did you do with the gun?"

"American movies were quite popular in my country before the government outlawed them. I disposed of it in a storm drain."

"A lot of men would've kept it. You know, in case Udo has revenge on his mind. You should watch your back."

"I have walked in the valley of death and I do not fear evil." Alfassi paused. "You look surprised, but that is because you are not familiar with the Qur'an. A passage in it states David was given the Psalms and they were inspired by Allah."

"Another question?"

"If you need to ask, who am I to stop you?"

"I'm told you carried me all the way to the hospital."

"In truth, you walked part of the way. I do not have an automobile so I could not drive you. I thought it quicker to go on foot than wait for an ambulance."

"How come you didn't stick around?"

"I am not a doctor. I am also not comfortable speaking with authorities. It is my intention to keep, as you say in America, a low profile."

Jack paused. "If you're worried I gave anyone your name, don't." Jack tapped the side of his head. "I got temporary amnesia."

"Thank you, but I worry not. My fate is already decided."

"If your reluctance has anything to do with your immigration status, say, an expired visa or even no visa at all, you should know that the investigation into Garza's murder has already turned up a person with a similar problem. I put her in touch with a lawyer. Any conversation you had with him would be strictly protected."

Alfassi studied Jack's face. If he was looking for a tell that Jack had a hidden agenda, he would not find it.

"Thank you for your concern, but my family and I were granted refugee status for humanitarian reasons. I, myself, have obtained all the necessary forms which entitle me to work."

"Don't you have to apply for permanent residency within one year?"

"Ah, the magical green card. The key to the promised land."

"My lawyer can help if you're having trouble securing it. His name is Cicero Broadshank."

Alfassi did not offer comment and Jack couldn't tell whether he'd already gotten one or not. Maybe the shopkeeper was holding out hope he and his children could return to their homeland someday.

"Now, may I ask you a question?" Alfassi said.

"Fire away."

"I am surprised that you knew it was me. You were not always conscious, and when you did speak you confused me with someone else."

"I took a few wallops to the noggin, that's for sure."

"It seems that you believed you were on a different journey. Who is Hark?"

"Brother from another mother. We grew up together. We've had a number of... let's call them adventures together."

"Is he the friend you spoke of who has been charged with Mr. Penny's murder?"

Jack nodded.

"The news reports his name as something different."

"Geraldo Martinez, but he goes by Hark because of his neck tattoo. The artist spelled his name with an *H* and left off the *o*.

Then he tried to dress it up with angel wings. Hark came about the nickname because of a Christmas carol."

"Yes, I have heard it playing in stores. I have the sense he is also familiar with war."

Jack sucked his teeth. "He did two tours in Afghanistan."

"Fighting Muslims."

"I think he'd say he was defending the country against terrorists. But, look, one thing is for certain. Hark's not anti-Muslim. The only thing he is anti is injustice and unfair odds. He's as loyal and honorable as they come."

"I did not suggest otherwise."

"And I don't suggest I know anything about the world you come from either. I'm sure the news we get doesn't even scratch the surface."

Alfassi dusted another row of women's shoes. "You spoke as if you witnessed a terrible tragedy."

"I did. Sounds like I was reliving a dream I can't shake. A nightmare, really. A year ago I watched my daughter's mother die. I blame myself for letting it happen even though she dealt the card herself."

"Your wife is your daughter's stepmother?"

"Yes."

"Perhaps the tragedy was a blessing. Who are we to question Allah's ways? One woman dies and another receives a daughter."

"The same could be said for me. I didn't know about Zita the first three years of her life."

"I pray your daughter did not see her mother perish."

"Zita was in Argentina at the time, so no, she didn't. It's a long story, but I had to fly down to get her. Hark went with me."

"Sometimes we are left with little choice when protecting our children from violence."

"I know you speak from experience. Surviving in a bombarded city. Trekking across mountains and desert."

"True, but Allah was my guide. And you, how do you find your way?"

Jack had turned his back on organized religion long ago, but that didn't mean he didn't have a moral compass. Even on the grift he abided by the golden rule that you can't cheat an honest man. While his north star had changed when he fell for Katie and children came into his life, he continued to believe a man's destiny was his own.

Alfassi seemed to sense he wasn't going to get an answer and so he asked another question. "I know how the journey you and I took turned out, praise be. But I am curious about the journey to rescue your daughter."

"Bottom line is Hark and I entered a house where she was being held by some bad guys. We encouraged them to understand there was no upside for them to stay there. No one died that day. My daughter got a new life and so did I."

"It was all in His hands. You are blessed."

Again, Jack did not contradict Alfassi's beliefs. Like anyone else's, he was entitled to them.

"Look, I've got to book, but how about Katie and I have you and the kids over for dinner one night."

Alfassi showed a trace of a smile. "That is most generous. We would be honored."

## 30

Jack was running on fumes. Any nutritional value of the milkshake was long gone. He chased another pain pill with a shot of espresso and lurched across the street to the Double Dice.

DD took one look at him and wordlessly poured a shot of mescal. Jack waved him off. "Doctor's orders."

"It's not for you." DD parodied a shudder and slammed the cactus juice down. "I hurt all over just looking at you. I heard you got worked over, but, man, what did you do to deserve such a beat down."

"I suppose everyone on the street knows by now."

"Cops taking blood samples from your doorway doesn't leave much room for imagination."

"I need to sit down before I fall down."

Jack didn't think he could handle a backless bar stool so he pulled a chair away from the nearest table and eased onto it like a bird settling on a newly laid egg.

"I don't know who did it so you're wasting your time asking," DD said.

"Not why I'm here. I found Valentine. I gave her Cicero

Broadshank's number. He can help straighten out her visa problem."

DD skated the shot glass around and said, "Where's she at?"

"A friend's."

"Is she coming back to work?" He made it sound as if he didn't care.

"I suppose that depends on you."

"Why me?"

"Whether you want her to."

"Why not? She's a good server. Good for business too."

"That the only reason?"

"Finding a good cocktail waitress can be a pain."

"That why you're acting so hard like you don't care what happened to her or where's she at?"

DD snorted. "Your head must be hurt worse than it looks."

"It's all you can do to keep from asking me to drive you there. You know what Katie says when I tell her I got to go on a trip? 'Good. How can I miss you if you never go away?' "

"Hey, McCoul. If I want love advice, I'll log into 7 Cups of Tea."

"The fact that you know that confirms you're crazy about her. You wouldn't have threatened to break Frankie Penny's arm if you weren't."

"Valentine told you about that?"

"And you got in Ricky Udo's face while you were at it."

"Udo's a punk. All that fight club shit he brags about? I hear most of his wins are because the other guy got paid to take a dive."

"You got proof?"

"I heard it more than once. One guy told me he got two hundred bucks for letting Udo land one on his chin. Made it real so when he hit the deck no one would think otherwise."

Jack sat up straighter. "Paying someone to throw a fight isn't to stroke your ego, it's to guarantee a payoff on a big bet. Oldest play in the book. Well, at least in the fight game."

DD twisted a moustache tip. "That talk about you being a con artist isn't all bullshit, is it?"

A memory bloomed among the rubble inside Jack's injured skull. It was no secret back in high school that Frank Penny Sr. made big donations to St. Joseph's so his son got a spot on the roster. But there was also a rumor that a powerhouse team in the West Catholic Athletic League was paid to pull a Black Sox in a play-off game. Not only did Frankie get served up fat ones every time he came up to bat, but right after, the losing school broke ground on a new diamond funded by an anonymous donor. Even an altar boy like Terry Dolan took to calling it Penny Fields.

Jack took a stab. "What do you know about Frankie's gambling problem?"

DD shrugged. "Not much. A bartender I hired who used to tend at the Indian casino up by Petaluma recognized him. He told me Frank Jr. was a favorite customer up there. Comped drinks, comped rooms, the whole nine yards they give the high rollers. You know they only do that because they lose big."

"*Moby Dick*. They're called whales for a reason."

"What do you expect for a kid whose old man gave him too much allowance and hired Udo to protect him."

Jack said, "That's what I thought at first too, but now I think it was the other way around."

"What do you mean?"

"Frankie was such a fuck up, his old man had to have someone keep an eye on him to protect the company brand."

"If that's true, getting himself killed was an epic fail on all fronts."

*Murder left a stain, no doubt about it,* Jack thought. Even if the victim was innocent, people always wondered. And their suspicion usually extended to the victim's family members and close friends alike.

"That guy you know who took a dive for Udo. Think you could ask him who paid him off?"

"I don't need to. He told me it was Frank Jr. He said he even boasted about it afterward."

"Your friend believe him?"

"He had no reason not to. All he cared about was whether or not the two hundred bucks was real. It turned out he had to spend it all and then some getting his jaw wired. He said it felt like Udo was hiding a sap in his fist when he punched him."

Jack stroked his bruised chin. "Tell me about it."

CICERO BROADSHANK WAS HOLDING court at the House of Prime Rib. Insiders called the Van Ness Avenue institution the Hopper, not because of its acronym, but because more energy was spent hopping from one powerbroker table to the next than chewing rare roast beef and downing martinis.

Jack threaded his way through a crowd of sports figures and politicians to join the portly lawyer at a booth whose location was as prime as the rib being personally served to him by the impeccably dressed septuagenarian owner.

"Jack, my boy," Broadshank bellowed. "You have been injured. Fear not, for I will secure for you a very handsome settlement. Do you know if the perpetrator is insured? If so, the purse fattens as we speak."

Jack appreciated the booth's cushioning and wiped the opioid-induced sweat that had gathered on his brow with a white linen napkin. "I got a different kind of payback for him in mind, but before we get to that, let's talk about Hark's preliminary."

"Of course, but I can see you need sustenance first." He turned to the proprietor. "A King Henry VIII cut with all the fixings for my young friend."

Broadshank said to Jack, "It is a generous portion to be sure, but a man of your athletic physique needs copious amounts of protein."

"A dish of Yorkshire pudding and creamed spinach is about all my jaw can handle at the moment."

"Ah, a judicious while delicious decision."

Jack said, "We're getting down to the eleventh hour here. Hark's prelim's tomorrow. Where do we stand?"

Broadshank tut-tutted. "It is important to remember that a preliminary hearing for a capital offense is not a trial. While the superior court hearing is open to the public, no jury is present. It is incumbent upon the State to make the case for probable cause, not prove guilt. The judge has two options. One, reject probable cause and dismiss the case outright, or two, affirm the prosecution's presentation and bind it over for trial. All Mr. Martinez is required to do is restate his innocence and reconfirm his original plea."

"But the State presents evidence, right?"

"Quite so. They will only call a couple of witnesses and present an overview of the forensics. I presume the arresting officers will testify along with a representative from the SFPD crime scene laboratory. It is all very routine."

"Depending on what they have, they could bury Hark."

"No one is burying anyone at this point. The matter very much remains in the initial phase."

"Will you question their witnesses?"

"Of course, but only in a most cursory fashion. I will cast some seeds of doubt in their testimony and the forensics findings."

"And which witnesses will you call?"

A waiter brought over another martini. Broadshank grasped the stemmed glass in his meaty fingers and gulped noisily.

"None, of course. That would be quite the juris *faux pax.*"

"Why not if a witness could discredit the entire case and stop it from going to trial?"

"You must temper your optimism as well as your enthusiasm. May I remind you I do have a rather sterling record of victories that recently topped three hundred and twelve."

If Broadshank hadn't been clutching his martini in one hand and a dinner roll the size of a softball in the other, Jack was sure he would've blown on his fingernails and shined them on the lapel of his very expensive Italian wool suit.

"Indulge me. Why no witnesses?"

"Because it is to my client's advantage that I use the preliminary hearing for intelligence gathering purposes. The prosecution will be required to expose the very foundation of their case, both structural support and cracks alike. Based on that, I can develop the most effective defense for destroying it at trial. Why use explosives when a tiny tap with a hammer and chisel will do?"

"You don't want to show all your cards so they can do the same."

"Precisely. The defense does not need to at this juncture. Ah, look. Here comes your Yorkshire pudding. Marvelous. Make sure they leave the gravy boat behind. I could drink it like soup."

The creamed spinach didn't make Jack feel like Popeye, but the puffy soufflé of eggs and flower topped with beef drippings did provide some fortitude.

He asked more questions. "They're going to prove probable cause, aren't they?"

"I am afraid so."

"And Hark's not going to get bail, is he?"

The lawyer's jowls flapped as he shook his head. "I believe I

may have inadvertently committed an informational oversight."
He gulped some more martini. "There has been a last-minute
change in judge scheduling. This happens not infrequently. At
any rate, I have been informed that the Right Honorable Judge
Horatio Chun will be presiding."

Jack lost whatever little appetite he had. "Hark's going to
wind up at San Bruno for another year for sure."

"Maybe not. While, legally, there is nothing to prevent the
State from delaying the trial until then, there appears to be a
somewhat dramatic shift in the district attorney's strategy."

"I don't like the sound of that."

"To be candid, neither did I when I first got wind of it.
Evidently, her poll numbers are not what her campaign
manager would like. Findings from focus groups point to negative sentiment among voters because of the two high profile
murders in the city that remain unresolved, namely the check
cashing store owner's and Frank Penny Jr.'s. Not only does this
failure to close the cases reflect badly on the police department,
but it also sheds a considerable shadow on the prosecutorial
department. Sympathy always lies with the victims."

"The Rolling Stones might disagree."

"What?"

"Never mind. Go on, what do you think will happen?"

"Since there appears to be little forward movement on the
Garza matter, yet a suspect has been arrested and charged in the
latter crime, the decision to request the State to speed not slow
our trial now seems imminent."

"She's going to roll the dice and hope it comes up with a
guilty verdict by election eve."

"In a manner of speaking, yes. Achieving a victory under a
rushed time table is always a tall order and, normally, that
proves beneficial to the defense. But the fact that the prosecution has agreed to her request and is pushing for it does give

cause for concern. What, exactly, do they have that bestows such confidence?"

Broadshank polished off his martini with a flourish. "Of course, we shall find that out tomorrow. The hearing is scheduled for after lunch. I presume you will be there."

"Front and center."

## 31

An earthquake tipping the scales at 5.1 jolted San Francisco at 2:33 in the morning. Car alarms shrieked, canned goods crashed to the floor, and a 115 kv transformer at a substation in the Bayshore blew, shooting a fireball one hundred feet into the sky. Jack didn't hear a thing. Didn't feel anything either, not the building shaking, not Katie getting out of bed, not Harry crying when books jitterbugged off a shelf. When Jack finally did open his eyes, the sun was burning off a cloak of morning fog and the city was starting another business as usual day.

"You missed all the excitement," Katie said when he wandered out to the kitchen. "The Hayward Fault reminded us who's boss."

"You mean the only mother more beautiful and stronger than you."

"Flattery will get you everywhere. Hungry?"

"As a bear coming out of hibernation."

"Grr. I'll make you a power shake. How does soy milk, wheat germ, banana, bok choy, and almond butter sound?"

"Don't suppose I could get a side of bacon and hash browns with that?"

"You are feeling better."

"True that. Want to play doctor?"

"Better hold onto your stethoscope, Watson. If we get too frisky, you could crack another rib."

"My little Nurse Ratched."

Katie chopped fruit and spooned ingredients into the blender as Jack checked his phone for incoming. The wonders never ceased. A voice mail from Wonder Boy was another first. Jack had never seen him touch the phone at the Pier.

He returned the call after Katie packed up the kids and took off for a visit to one of her gyms.

"I s-s-spoke to your old friend Jimmie Fang," Wonder Boy said. "He s-s-said Frank Penny Jr. was a regular at his Chinatown club. Jimmie s-s-said he bet big on everything he played. Hold'em, pai gow, blackjack, even roulette."

"I should've thought of calling the little Triad gangster myself. Maybe that concussion did knock some gray matter loose. DD Mitchell told me he has a bartender who used to work the Indian casinos. Remembers Frankie as a whale. He was also hedging bets on Ricky's fight club bouts by bribing opponents to take a dive."

"That can be a very dangerous undertaking. Perhaps s-s-someone who lost money exacted revenge."

"I think it was something else." Jack gave a CliffsNotes version of Valentine seeing the Raiderettes leading Frank Jr. into Osage Alley.

"Jimmie s-s-said he was carrying a lot of paper on Frank Jr. S-s-so much s-s-so that Frank tried s-s-signing over property deeds as collateral. Jimmie didn't accept, but he s-s-suspects a loan s-s-shark or two might have."

"Most likely it was the Russians out of the Sunset District.

Daddy would've gotten pretty pissed if he found that out. The only thing Frank Sr. finds more irreplaceable than his fair-haired son is land. As the saying in real estate goes, they aren't making any more."

St. Joseph's dominated a corner of the Mission District. Its bell tower, stained glass, and heavy wooden doors indicated sanctuary lay within the thick walls, but Jack knew the offer of redemption was not without a price. Father Bernardus kicked off every school day with a fiery sermon extolling the dire consequences of not adhering to the commandments. He added his own list of thou-shall-nots to the original ten. Jack used the time to figure out how to break the rules without getting caught.

Climbing the granite steps to the church's entrance led him to recall one Good Friday when his class was instructed to reenact the carrying of the cross. They fashioned a life-size replica out of salvaged redwood beams and took turns hauling the heavy timber up Dolores Street. When they finally staggered onto the church's grounds, they dug a hole in the middle of the ballfield and erected it.

The pitcher of that game now sat in a pew inside the darkened nave. Jack slid beside him.

"How's it going, Terry? You get a chance to confess your doubts about the department to the good *padre* yet?"

"Do me a favor and don't blaspheme in here," the homicide cop said as he kept his eyes glued to the altar where he'd lit candles and assisted Father Bernardus all through high school. "Your message said you had something new on the Garza killing. What is it?"

"Remember the time we planted that redwood crucifix in center field? It left a huge dip. Mike Shanahan was chasing down a sacrifice fly and tripped in it. Broke his ankle. Father Bernardus said it was God's way of punishing us for losing to Riordan the week before."

"What's that have to do with Garza?"

"I remember another ball game too. The play-off game for the league championship when Frankie Penny went three for four. It was like the pitcher was setting it on a batting tee for him."

Terry sighed. "It all gets back to the Penny murder, doesn't it? It that what this is, another desperate attempt to get me to do something for Hark? Well, it's a little late in the game since the preliminary is in a few hours."

"Everyone knew Frankie's old man paid off the other school to take a dive. Well, it turns out the pippin doesn't fall far from the tree. Junior was using the same approach when it came to gambling. Namely, paying fight club guys to hit the canvas against Ricky Udo."

"So, now you're wrapping in the witness who overheard Frank Jr. arguing with Hark the night of the murder."

"*Allegedly* on both accounts. Betting on fight club bouts wasn't all. Frankie developed a real jones. But like most gamblers, the only thing he was really good at was losing. He got in so deep he had to borrow from the *Bratva* boys. He signed over property deeds as collateral."

"And now you want me to believe a local Russian gang is responsible for Frank Jr.'s death? That beating certainly sparked your imagination."

"They didn't kill Frankie. Udo did."

Terry groaned. "And why would he do that?"

"To keep Frankie's mouth shut."

"I don't suppose you have any proof to go along with this fantasy of yours."

"Ricky's gun. I took it off him. He came looking for it.

Seemed pretty anxious to get it back." Jack pointed at his temple. The bandage was gone but the sutures showed.

"You're forgetting something. Something very important. It's called the facts. Frank Penny Jr. wasn't shot. He was beaten to death."

"By Udo. And Udo's gun? It's going to be a match for the slugs they took out of Garza."

It was as if hot wax from a votive candle dripped on the cop's head. "What are you talking about?"

"Frank Sr. originally hired Udo as a rent collector. Udo graduated to frightening tenants into breaking their leases so Penny could kick them out for higher paying tenants or when he needed to clear a building and build a new one. Udo did such a good job, Frank Sr. assigned him to keep his problem child out of trouble."

"How do you know this?"

"Used my head." Jack gestured at his battered skull again and grinned. "Stay with me here. Garza had already been threatened before after he'd balked at a 400 percent rent increase. He even went to city hall and complained. When his shop got vandalized, he still didn't back down. Udo was told to put a real scare into him. What's a shopkeeper most frightened of? A stickup. Frankie decides to go along. He and Udo make it look real. They put on masks, spray paint the cameras, and stick a gun in Garza's face and tell him to open the safe. When he does, everything changes. Maybe Garza puts up a fight. Maybe Frankie sees all that cash and decides he can use it to pay off some of his gambling IOUs. Either way, Udo shoots Garza. Twice in the chest. The tap to the head was to make sure. You work Robbery so you tell me. When does a stickup artist waste time or lead doing that?"

"You need proof. All you have is speculation."

"I got Udo's gun. You do the fingerprinting. Do the ballistics.

So, back to Frankie. The day after the Garza murder, Frankie's down at the Gold Rush folding big bills into Valentine Song's G-string like there's no tomorrow. Before then he'd never tipped her anything larger than a Washington. He follows her to the Double Dice and tries doing the same. Suddenly, he's Mr. Bigshot. Udo gets nervous that Frankie's calling too much attention to himself. Either he decides to clean up his own mess or his boss orders him to."

Terry snorted so loud an old lady dressed in black praying in the front pew wheeled around and shot him the evil eye.

"Even if I did believe Udo and Frank Jr. robbed Garza, which I don't, you expect me to believe Frank Penny Sr. had his own son murdered?"

"I found out that Senior's gone all in on a huge redevelopment project aimed at the Mission. I can show you the plans. He can't risk jeopardizing his investment because Junior acted like a dumb shit. And he sure doesn't want to risk a hit to the family name. Frank Sr.'s reserved seat in the front pew here and Friday night dinners with the archbishop? Kiss them goodbye."

"If I tried telling this to my captain, I wouldn't even be able to land a job with TSA."

"Play it right and you could be your own captain. We can link the gun to Udo and Udo to Frankie's murder. You'd get two solveds."

"*We?* We don't link anything together. I shouldn't be talking to you in the first place."

"You came to me, remember? I'm throwing you a bone, and you know it. Hark's innocent. If you don't help him, they'll crucify him."

The homicide cop grew silent. His gaze went back to the altar and the figure of Christ hanging on the cross.

"Okay. Hand over Udo's gun."

"Not until after you testify at the prelim this afternoon. I'll get word to Broadshank to call you as a witness. You say you've uncovered new evidence about Garza's murder that has a direct correlation to Frankie's death and it clears Hark."

Terry jabbed a finger into Jack's chest. "I can run you in for obstruction. Give me that weapon."

"Go ahead and arrest me. But you know that's not going to help you solve Garza's killing, much less Frankie's. Without closing either case, Erick Berlin is going to continue to ride you all the way to the mayor's office. Forget TSA. You'll be lucky if they let you drive a meter reader scooter."

The cop hesitated. When he did, Jack slipped out of the pew and disappeared as quickly as he used to when ditching morning sermons.

## 32

A 1964 Chevy Impala the color of a Golden Gate sunset was idling out front of Jack's loft, the rumble coming from the lowrider's twin silver tail pipes as familiar as a best friend's laugh. Jack couldn't count all the hours he'd spent in the shotgun bucket, cruising the streets of San Francisco. But as much as he wished, it wouldn't be the owner sitting behind the chrome chain-link steering wheel.

Jack had to crouch to look through the open passenger window. Vinny Vargas seemed small in the driver's seat. Benicio Tuxtla loomed menacingly in the back.

"You don't look like the photo of the driver I hailed," Jack said.

"What? I ain't no ant," Vinny said.

"Did Hark drop the keys to his pride and joy when the cops hauled him off or did you hotwire it?"

The kid hunched over the wheel. "Come on. We got to get a move on or we'll be late."

"For what?"

"Hark's trial. We're going with you."

"No way you're getting near the Hall."

"Get in the fuckin' whip," Tuxtla growled. The effort triggered a coughing fit.

"Well, don't expect a five-star from me," Jack said as he opened the door and slid into the bucket.

Vinny stomped on the gas and the pipes spit flames and the spinning rear wheels shot an acrid rooster tail of black smoke. He flipped a U-turn and roared up Brannan.

"We need to agree on some ground rules before we get there," Jack said. "First, no shouting, no swearing, no smoking in the courtroom."

"Is that supposed to be some kinda joke?" Tuxtla wheezed.

"Second, Hark's lawyer knows what he's doing, so don't interrupt him, don't threaten him, and don't talk to him before or after. He'll bill me for it."

Tuxtla was sitting forward so his head was nearly on Jack's shoulder. His breath smelled like he'd swallowed turpentine. "You think I don't know this shit already? I been where Hark's at plenty times."

"And look how that turned out," Jack muttered.

"What'd you say, *pendejo*?"

"Third, the place is going to be filled with cops. If you got a grudge with one or if they have one with you, or if there's a warrant out for you, don't get out of the car."

Vinny pushed yellows and weaved through traffic. He didn't seem to know there was such a thing as a brake pedal. "They're going to kick him loose, yeah?"

Jack sucked his teeth. It tasted like spoiled meat. One of the temporary caps must be leaking. "The lawyer defending him will do his best. Anything's possible."

"But Hark didn't do it. You said so. So they can't find him guilty."

"The man can do whatever the man wants," Tuxtla growled.

"Lock you up, throw away the key. Strap you in the green room and pump it full of gas."

"It's not a trial," Jack said. "All the prosecution is trying to do is convince the judge there's probable cause."

"Whatever," Vinny said. "But he could not be convinced, the judge, yeah?"

"That'll depend on a couple of things."

Tuxtla coughed again. The sound of phlegm trapped inside a bony chest rattled in Jack's ear. "What happened to your face? Your wife smack you around?"

"I can see why Hark's *abuelita* isn't your number one fan. No, this was courtesy of a punk named Ricky Udo."

Jack watched Tuxtla in the rearview mirror. The man's gray face showed recognition. "I heard of him."

"How so?"

"It's the name of the *güero* who ordered a hit on my... on Hark. Someone on the inside told me."

"A dude called the shop asking for him." Vinny said it with a boast. "Remember? I'm the cutoff. I got word to Benicio and gave him the call back number."

Tuxtla said, "The caller said he was in San Bruno. Said he overheard some corn-feds with the Aryan Brotherhood talking in the yard. The AB didn't ask why Udo ordered it done, just took the money for it and carried out the hit. Guess they didn't figure on Hark being so *fuerte*."

Jack looked out the window. He wasn't watching for addresses or pedestrians. He was looking at all the plays he'd put on the board. Whatever he said now would have aftershocks as surely as the recent earthquakes. He turned toward Tuxtla.

"Ricky Udo came after me because I took a gun off him. He wanted to make sure it didn't get tied to him because of something he did."

"What's the *something*?"

He thought of the line his old man used when Jack discovered he'd gone from filching valuables from burning houses while fighting fires to coming back later and loading up the truck. *In for a penny, boyo, in for a pound.*

"Udo killed a guy who ran a money wire shop. Frankie Penny was in on the stickup. Udo had his muscle take Frankie to an alley where he killed him to keep his mouth shut."

Tuxtla sat back in the seat. "The punk framed Hark and then ordered him hit to make it stick."

"Maybe you're on to something," Jack said.

"All we have to do is tell the cops and Hark'll get off and this Udo dude will fry, yeah?" Vinny said.

"In a perfect world, yes," Jack said.

Tuxtla coughed again. It seemed to prevent him from saying anything more.

THEY COULDN'T PARK ANYWHERE near the Hall. Though it was only a hearing, the media was treating it as if it were the murder trial of the century. News vans with fully erect satellite periscopes were stationed bumper-to-bumper. Double-parked food trucks did a lively business. Camera crews roped off valuable real estate on the sidewalk to ensure their on-air talent would have the imposing granite building as a backdrop. The line of people waiting to pass through security wrapped around the block.

Jack ushered his unlikely wards to the front of the line. "Look sicker," he whispered and stuck his arm under Tuxtla's as if propping him up. He motioned for Vinny to do the same. He hailed a guard. "We got a disabled man here."

When the guard eyeballed them, Tuxtla coughed and held

out a handkerchief spotted with blood. The guard stepped back. "Go ahead. You still got to empty your pockets."

Jack led the way through the metal detector. He held his breath as the old con followed and only exhaled when no alarm screamed. The elevator was jammed as they ascended to the superior court floor. The front rows of the oak paneled court-room were already filled, but Jack found three seats halfway back and took the one in the middle.

"What now?" Vinny asked.

"We wait until the judge arrives. He's probably still eating lunch in his chambers."

"Which one's our lawyer?"

"He's not here yet either. I'm sure he's meeting with Hark to go over stuff."

"And the dudes want to hang it on him?"

"The prosecution team. They're the ones up there in the front wearing dark suits. Two men and a woman."

"What's with those lame haircuts?" Vinny said.

A waft of turpentine floated by. Tuxtla leaned over and said, "Who they got as wits?"

"They'll probably call one of the cops who made the arrest, maybe two, and someone from the crime lab."

Tuxtla spit in his handkerchief. "Dogs don't lie as much as pigs. They only say what the DA tells them to say."

"Remember what I said coming over."

Tuxtla put his hands on his knees. The woman sitting next to him glanced over and saw the tattooed knuckles. She tilted her head to read the letters and abruptly changed seats.

Cicero Broadshank strode into the courtroom and straight to the opposing counsel. He greeted them in a loud but disdainful baritone. "Last chance to save your integrity and drop this charade."

They bunched closer and offered no reply.

Before sitting down, Broadshank glanced over his shoulder. Jack met his gaze with a nod, but the lawyer was wearing his game face. If he'd read the text Jack sent earlier outlining his meeting with Terry Dolan and to call him as a witness, he didn't acknowledge it. There was nothing more Jack could do but sit back and watch.

"All rise!" the bailiff called.

Judge Horatio Chun made a theatrical appearance from behind a screen. The heels of his cowboy boots drummed the steps as he climbed to the bench. As if choreographed, the side door opened and a pair of sheriff's deputies ushered in Hark. Broadshank had chalked up an early victory. Hark was dressed in street clothes. He wasn't manacled either. Appearances were everything in a courtroom.

The next few minutes were spent reading the charges, dispensing the ground rules of the pre-trial hearing, and reconfirming Geraldo Santiago Martinez's plea of not guilty.

Jack caught another poisonous whiff as Tuxtla leaned in chose. "So that's him. He looks strong. *Muy guapo.* I can tell they ain't broke his spirit. That's good."

Somebody shushed him from the row behind. Vinny turned around and gave them the finger.

Jack focused on the front row. San Francisco's district attorney wasn't there, but he knew she'd be following the proceedings on closed-circuit TV. Supervisor Erick Berlin wasn't present either. Nor was Terry. Jack held out hope that Broadshank had connected with the cop. He told himself that witnesses rarely sat in the courtroom until called.

The lead for the prosecution's team was a short man with a fringe of oily hair that flopped over his ears. He held a yellow legal tablet and referred to it often as he spoke. After delivering his opening about how the State was going to prove beyond all reasonable doubt that there was a just and probable cause for advancing the case to trial, he called his first witness.

Officer William Talbott had a dark brush cut salted with gray and a matching moustache. His uniform was crisply pressed and the badge on his chest was polished to a high gleam. He swore to give the whole truth and nothing but the truth. He maintained eye contact and spoke in a deliberative manner.

"Officer Talbott," the prosecutor said, "You were in your patrol car driving down Mission Street when alerted by an Officer Robert Chavez that he was in pursuit of a suspect on Osage Alley. Please describe how you responded."

"Officer Chavez and I agreed to perform a box maneuver to apprehend the fleeing suspect. I turned onto Twenty-Fourth Street and blocked Osage Alley with my unit while Chavez continued to push the suspect toward me. In doing so, we could use the adjacent buildings and our units to contain the suspect's movements."

"Did the plan work?"

"Negative. Prior to reaching my location, the suspect took evasive action. Officer Chavez alerted me to the situation. It was at this point I saw the suspect run across Twenty-Fourth Street where it intersects with Bartlett Avenue. Bartlett is one block west parallel to Osage. The suspect then proceeded westerly on Twenty-Fourth Street."

"Did you give pursuit?"

"Affirmative. The suspect turned right onto Valencia and ran in a northerly direction. He turned right again at Twenty-Second Street. I pursued him into a parking lot near that intersection. The lot is adjacent to a building. The suspect dropped from sight, but the only place he could have gone was inside the building."

"Did you follow him into the building?"

"Not immediately. I called for backup. Officer Chavez joined me. Dispatch then confirmed the original 911 involved a homicide. At that point, the suspect presented a clear and present danger to anyone inside the building. We continued our pursuit to protect their safety and welfare."

"And did you locate anyone inside the building?"

"Affirmative. We encountered the suspect. We placed him under arrest."

"Is that person presently in this room?"

"Affirmative. He is the gentleman standing between the two sheriff's deputies."

"Thank you, Officer Talbott. Nothing further, your Honor."

Cowboy Chun was swiveling in his high-back chair as he listened. "Counselor for the defense. Is it your intention to cross?"

"If it pleases the court," Broadshank said. "Officer Talbott, how long have you been with the San Francisco Police Department?"

"I graduated from the Academy ten years and three months ago and have been on active duty ever since."

"My, that is certainly a long tenure. During that time have you ever participated in a high-speed pursuit on city streets prior to the night in question?"

Talbott hesitated, his alarm bells triggered by the emphasis of *high-speed*. The City had recently been forced to shell out one million dollars to a pedestrian who'd been struck by a police car responding to a bank heist.

"As a patrol officer, I receive regular driving training."

"That is not what I asked. Have you ever participated in a high-speed pursuit before?"

"No, but I have undergone extensive training. At no time did I exceed the 25-mile-per-hour speed limit on city streets in the night in question."

"Well, I am glad you know the city's speed limit. I wish the same could be said for our garbage collectors and bus drivers."

An undercurrent of chuckles swept the courtroom. Chun banged his gavel.

Broadshank said, "So, Officer Talbott, is it your sworn testimony that you never reached twenty-six miles per hour during the pursuit?"

"Affirmative."

"Are you certain? Let me rephrase the question. Are you testifying that you never exceeded twenty-five miles per hour?"

Talbott paused again. Jack could see the cop calculating as he tried to stay one step ahead of Broadshank. "It would be more accurate to say I averaged twenty-five miles per hour during the pursuit."

"Ah, so to make sure that I understand you correctly. You were driving your patrol car at an average of twenty-five miles per hour while chasing an individual who was on foot. Is that correct?"

"Affirmative."

"What's he getting at?" Tuxtla whispered.

"Watch and learn," Jack whispered back.

Broadshank drew close to the witness box. "And while averaging the speed limit over the course of several city blocks, were you able to apprehend the individual before you reached the parking lot?"

"Negative. It wasn't until he entered the building."

"I must say, it would appear the subject of your pursuit is unusually athletic. Few humans on Earth can run an average of twenty-five miles per hour for any sustained length. Even the great Usain Bolt who reached a top speed of 27.8 miles per hour did so for only a distance of one hundred meters, which is half the length of a city block. Yet this individual maintained nearly that speed for several full city blocks."

The undercurrent of chuckles turned into laughter. Chun had to bang the gavel again.

"Objection," the prosecutor shouted. "Calls for speculation."

"I think you mean to say, 'calls for incredulousness!' " Broadshank fired back in his most bombastic tone.

Chun kept pounding. "Order. May I remind both counselors that this is a preliminary hearing only. No showboating, Mr. Broadshank. Do you have anything else?"

"Certainly, your Honor." He focused on the patrol cop again. "Did you ever lose sight of the individual you were pursuing?"

Talbott hesitated. "I was driving on city streets with lights and siren, but the pursuit required entering and exiting intersections, and so I made sure those intersections and crosswalks were clear of pedestrians and oncoming vehicles."

"In other words, you took your eyes off the suspect."

"Objection. The defense is making a conclusion," the prosecutor said.

The judge nodded. "Sustained. Is there a question in there, counselor?"

"Was there ever a time during the pursuit when the individual was not in your direct line of sight?"

Again, Talbott hesitated. "Yes, but only briefly for a few times."

Broadshank hid a smile. "Is it not true that in your previous testimony, you stated that you did not see the individual you were pursuing enter the building adjacent to the parking lot?"

"It's the only place he could have gone," Talbott said.

"Yes or no, officer. Did you see with your own eyes the individual you were chasing enter the building?"

"No, but there's nowhere else he could've gone."

"Let the record show the officer stated 'no' to the question of did he see anyone enter the building."

Broadshank drew a theatrical breath. "Now, prior to entering the automobile paint and body shop owned by my client for several years, have you ever seen him before?"

"Negative."

"What about the night in question? Did you see his face prior to your entrance into his place of business?"

Talbott paused. "I saw a man run across Twenty-Fourth Street from Bartlett. I pursued him to the parking lot."

"Did you see his face?"

"No."

"I would like to state for the record, Officer Talbott said 'no' to the question of did he see the face of the individual he was pursuing."

"Move it along, counselor," Chun warned from the bench.

"Officer Talbott, is the man you apprehended and arrested in this courtroom?"

"Affirmative."

"Would you please indicate him?"

The cop pointed at Hark. Hark remained stone-faced.

"Let the record show that Officer Talbott pointed to Mr. Geraldo Santiago Martinez, U.S. Army retired."

"Did Mr. Martinez resist or try to flee when you apprehended him in his own building?"

"Officer Chavez and I didn't give him a chance."

"How did you apprehend him?"

"We entered the premises, located him, and arrested him."

"How did you enter the building?"

"Through the front door?"

"Did you knock before entering?"

"Yes."

"Did you identify yourself as police."

"Yes."

"Did anyone answer the door?"

"No."

"What did you do then?"

"We went in."

"Was the door locked?"

"Affirmative."

"Then how did you get in?"

"We used an enforcer."

"What is an enforcer?"

"It's a manual battering ram used to breech a door."

"Was music playing inside the building?"

"I believe it was."

"And where did you find Mr. Martinez?"

"In the can. The bathroom. He was in the bathroom."

"Where was the bathroom located? In the front of the building, the middle, or the rear?"

"In the back."

"All right, the bathroom was in the back of the building opposite of where you entered. Could it be that given the bathroom's remote location and given the loud music that was playing, Mr. Martinez did not hear you knock?"

The prosecutor pounced. "Objection. Calls for speculation."

"Sustained. Move along, Mr. Broadshank," Chun said.

"What was Mr. Martinez doing when you entered the bathroom?"

"He was bandaging his hand. His knuckles were all scraped up. The kind of scrapes you get from beating a man to death."

Broadshank turned to the judge. "Your Honor, really. I realize this is only a preliminary hearing, but such biased comments are not only prejudicial, they are grossly misleading and a miscarriage of justice. I request they be stricken from the record."

Cowboy Chun grimaced. "Officer Talbott, please keep your opinions to yourself and only state the facts."

Broadshank continued, "Did Mr. Martinez resist arrest or

attempt to flee when you announced yourself? I assume you did announce you were law enforcement personnel."

"We called out and we had our guns drawn. Not many people resist when they have several weapons pointed at them."

Broadshank cleared his throat before booming, "Let the record state the officer said 'no' to the question of resistance or flight. Judge Chun, please, I must request that the officer's opinion be struck from the record yet again."

The lawyer didn't wait for a response. He turned back to the witness box.

"Now, Officer Talbott, is the man you arrested here in the courtroom?"

"I already pointed him out."

"Would you do so again please?"

Talbott hooked a finger in Hark's direction.

Broadshank said. "I am afraid pointing is not adequate. For the written record, would you please describe him? Height, weight, build, and so forth."

"The suspect is close to six feet. He looks to go at least 250 pounds. Maybe 275."

"Would you say that Mr. Martinez is a rather large gentleman of considerable weight and height?"

"He's bigger than most."

"Most *what*?" Tuxtla grumbled.

"Easy," Jack said under his breath.

Broadshank turned so he was half facing the audience, "So, you are pointing to a man of considerable size, who, according to your own sworn testimony, can outrun an eight-time gold medal winner."

Laughter ripped through the audience. Vinny raised his hand to high-five Tuxtla. "Cop's lying about everything."

Jack said, "Hark never runs. He stands his ground. Always."

"*Muy macho.* I respect that," Tuxtla said.

"Really, Officer," Broadshank continued. "Do you expect the judge or anybody here to believe Mr. Martinez could outrun your patrol car? A man, by the way, who sustained grievous injury during combat while defending this country in Afghanistan. A man whose nation honored his heroism by bestowing upon him not one, but two Purple Hearts. Do you really Officer Talbott?"

The prosecutor jumped up and shouted. "Objection!"

Before Chun could rule, Broadshank said, "Nothing further, your Honor."

The judge pounded his gavel. "We'll take a fifteen-minute recess."

## 33

Benicio Tuxtla was looking more and more like a man in need of an oxygen tank. Vinny Vargas was nearly coming out of his oversized white leather high tops as he paced the hallway outside the courtroom. Jack ignored them both and went in search of Cicero Broadshank. He found him in a men's room reserved for court officials. The lawyer had finished his business and was holding his hands under a running faucet like a surgeon readying for a heart transplant.

"Jack, my boy. Come to sing my praises, I expect?"

"Sing and whine. Nice job painting Hark versus a V-8, but what happened with Terry Dolan? His testimony would have made reasonable doubt a slam dunk."

"Regrettably, the detective did not embrace my invitation to do so."

"You didn't subpoena him?"

"The wheels of justice do not move with such alacrity. I did not receive your advisement of this development with sufficient time to obtain approval of a summons or serve it. Nor was there any allowance to request a stay, even though I believe such an entreaty would have fallen on deaf ears given the superior court's inflexibility to alter its schedule, not to mention the district attorney's pressure for pressing full speed ahead."

"Maybe it won't matter. Cowboy Chun can't rule for probable cause after you poked holes in Talbott's testimony big enough to drive a patrol car through."

"Predicting judges is difficult at best. Should my exposure of the faults in the officer's recollection of the night in question not produce the outcome I am looking for today, I do find comfort in knowing that I can build upon the absurdity of the chase particulars should the matter proceed to a juried trial."

"I guess we'll know any minute."

"Three to be precise," Broadshank said as he glanced at his wristwatch while drying his hands.

Jack headed back to the courtroom. He stopped to collect Vinny and Tuxtla on the way. The ex-con was laboring so Jack asked him if he needed a hand.

"If I'm breathing I'm walking," he said. "What the suit said about him, Hark. That he got shot in the war. That right?"

"As rain."

"I respect that. The *hombre's* got sand. Real sand. You got to honor that. I mean, you know, him doing that and all. Fighting over there. Being all loyal and all. I respect that. Like, makes you proud."

"We better get in there before someone takes our seats."

"Like to see them try," Vinny said.

No one did and so they settled back into their chairs. They didn't have to wait long. The bailiff called, "All rise!" Chun swept in, his black robes rustling. The side door opened and the deputies brought in Hark.

Chun cut right to the chase. "In the matter of the State of California versus Geraldo Santiago Martinez, to the question of whether there is probable cause that a crime of murder in the first degree was committed upon Frank Penny Jr., I find for the State. To the question of whether there is probable cause that the defendant, Geraldo Santiago Martinez, is the person responsible for the crime of murder in the first degree committed upon Frank Penny Jr., I find for the State. I hereby submit this case to trial court. The case manager will coordinate scheduling trial proceedings with opposing counsel. This hearing is now closed."

Groans and cheers followed the banging of the gavel. The deputies rushed Hark through the side door before he could say a word. Broadshank shook his mane of white hair.

Jack sat back in his chair. The ruling came so fast, it felt as if all the air had been sucked from the room.

"What the hell just happened?" Vinny said.

"The judge ruled against him." The words came out of his mouth, but to Jack they didn't sound like his own.

Vinny's face twisted. "Can he do that?"

"He just did."

Jack looked over at Tuxtla, knowing that he more than anyone knew what the penalty would be if Hark was found guilty of killing another human. Tuxtla sat rigidly. He didn't cough. He didn't say a word. But the look in his eyes did.

Vinny started stomping his feet. The oversized shoes sounded like a timpani drum at the end of a symphony. "I can't believe it. Lying cop. Crooked judge."

Jack put a quieting hand on the kid's knee. "Let's get out of here."

He led them down the hall and into the elevator. Vinny was shaking. Tuxtla rode looking straight ahead.

They had to squeeze past a crowd of reporters doing stand-ups as the they exited the Hall. Shauna Rhames was interviewing Erick Berlin. The supervisor wore a serious expression as he answered her questions. Jack didn't need to hear them to know he was making a pitch for community policing and afford-able housing to make the world a better place.

"I'll drive," Jack said when they reached the Impala lowrider.

Vinny started to protest, but Tuxtla put a warning finger out and held it up to the kid's face. "Respect."

They were quiet as Jack drove back to Hark's shop. He parked in the lot and they all got out. Jack gave the keys to Vinny and the kid walked with his head down as he went to unlock the front door.

"I'm going over to the restaurant to tell *Abuelita* what went down," Jack said to Tuxtla.

"Nothing you can say will make that old *bruja* feel good."

"All I can do is tell her the truth. It was only the prelim. They still have to prove Hark did it in a juried trial. But the longer he waits, the more opportunities Ricky Udo has for taking another run at him."

"The suit, he didn't know what you know, about what that *puta* did to the check cashing guy and Penny Jr.?"

"He got the 411 too late. Now he'll have to hold onto it until the trial."

Tuxtla coughed. When he caught his breath, he said, "The cops, the politicians, they already made up their minds to pin it on Hark. They're doing what the rich man told them."

"Maybe." Jack let it hang.

"Life in the pen, maybe the gas, for something he didn't do? He don't deserve that. And he sure don't deserve getting shanked."

Jack nodded.

The ex-con wiped flecks of bloody spittle off his lips and shoved the handkerchief in his back pocket. "That gun you took off Udo, you give it back to him?"

"No way. But he certainly wants it. He'd probably pay anything for it."

"I bet he would." And Tuxtla walked away without looking back.

## 34

J ack watched the battery icon swell as the charger pumped juice into his phone. He'd nearly drained it while on hold, waiting to get a call through the San Bruno jail switchboard. He never did reach Hark.

Dusk followed the sun as it sailed over Twin Peaks and plunged into the cold waters of the Pacific behind the Farallon Islands. The tide reversed course and rushed back under the most beautiful bridge in the world. Inbound freighters and fishing boats took advantage of the free ride and seabirds followed. Rush hour traffic clogged city streets and the onramps to Highway 101. A street busker laid down Jerry Garcia riffs on an electric Fender plugged into a battery-powered amplifier he toted on a Radio Flyer red wagon.

The rising tide brought with it more than fresh seawater, boats, and birds. It carried an impending sense of time running out. Jack's post-hearing call with Cicero Broadshank did little to stem the feeling. The lawyer confirmed that at the same time Hark was being bussed back to his cell, the prosecution success-fully persuaded the case manager to assign a trial date before the election. Broadshank also got a heads-up from his moles inside the attorney general's office that a plan was afoot to delay providing him with the discovery packet until the last possible moment. That meant he would have little time to review the evidence before trial.

"I assure you that packet will have as many holes in it as a slice of aged Emmentaler," the lawyer told Jack over the noise of cutlery clinking on bone china.

Jack stared out the window, searching for answers among the dying light. He'd put a lot of balls in the air in his quest to free his friend. Sooner or later one was going to fall. The trick was to anticipate which one and when, and know whether to let it crash to the ground or catch it and keep juggling.

Zita's chatter followed by Katie's voice and Harry's gurgle pulled him from his thoughts. The little girl skipped toward him.

"Katie says the next time the Giants are here we can go to a game. I want to get a baseball shirt that says *Gigantes*. I saw a boy wearing one. It had *Gigantes* on the front and *Marichal* on the back above the number twenty-seven. What is a *Marichal*?"

"Not a what, a who. Juan Marichal was one of the greatest pitchers ever."

"He doesn't play anymore?"

"Not for a long time, but Giants fans will never forget him."

"Juan Marichal is a Spanish name. Was he from Argentina too?"

"The Dominican Republic."

"I'm going to go look for it in the book with all the maps." And she skipped away.

Katie was bouncing Harry in her arms. "I can't believe we haven't been to a game yet. Especially you. You didn't even make it to opening day, and you never miss."

"Been a little busy," he said.

"Don't blame it on the children," she said.

"I wasn't blaming anyone. I meant busy with other stuff. You know, Hark."

She put the baby down on the floor. He immediately went to work trying to roll over. Jack thought of a turtle.

Katie said, "I'm sorry it didn't go well. But there's still the trial."

"CB thinks he can win, but the way things are going..."

"You don't want to wait that long, do you?"

Jack didn't answer.

"And you're going to keep trying to do something about it," she said.

"Yeah, I even asked your old boyfriend for help."

"Emphasis on the word *old*. But I have to admit, I do like it a little bit when you act jealous." She gave him a coy look.

"I'll keep that in mind."

"Is Terry helping?"

"He didn't today, but I got to tell you, he's not exactly Mr. Job Satisfaction these days. Kind of wonder how long he'll stay being a cop, though I can't imagine him ever doing anything else."

Katie frowned. "I feel sorry for him. I've read the news. I'm surprised, really."

"By what?"

"By the way Supervisor Belin has been acting. I really liked him. He was doing so much for disadvantaged families, the homeless and justice issues, but now he seems fixated on doing whatever he can to become mayor, even if it means using people like Terry."

"And you thought con artists were selfish."

"I did and I still do. That's why I'm glad you're not doing that anymore." When he didn't say anything, she drew close to him. "You aren't, are you? Tell me you're not."

"I never conned you and I never will."

She cocked her head. "What kind of answer is that?"

"The only kind you're going to get." And he kissed her.

## 35

Sirens wailed. The thwap-thwap of police helicopters concussed dully. The beams from their search lights sliced back and forth over the Mission District. The commotion drew Jack to the bedroom's open window. One of the balls had dropped.

It took him minutes to speed there in the Prius. Mission Street was already blocked off by police cars. Snipers were flattening themselves behind tripods on rooftops. Troops of black-helmeted cops wearing knee pads and tactical boots were getting a briefing from a SWAT commander sporting a Glock 9mm Velcroed to the front of his Kevlar vest. An Action News van was parked in front of the barricade. The downdraft from the choppers was wreaking havoc on the reporter's hairdo as she delivered a stand-up.

"This is Shauna Rhames with breaking news. I'm here in the Mission District and as you can see behind me police have cordoned off a building where shots fired have been reported. The situation is still unfolding, the information sketchy, but we've been told there are multiple casualties and hostages."

Jack looked at the building SWAT was preparing to storm. It

wasn't his. It was the headquarters of Frank Penny & Son Real Estate.

Rhames led her crew toward the huddle of SWAT cops. Jack snatched a boom mike from the back of the news van and followed. A beat cop tried to intercept them.

"This is an unsecured location, ma'am. You need to turn back."

The reporter shoved her chin at him and the cameraman followed suit with his lens. "What's your name, officer?"

"Uh, you can't be here," he said.

"Who's your commanding officer?"

The cop turned tail. Jack stayed right behind Rhames as she pushed her way through the team of black-clad cops.

"Commander, what's happening inside the building?" she demanded.

The SWAT leader had a shaved head the shape of a bullet. "You got some balls coming in here, lady. Now get out of here before you get hurt."

"I'm Shauna Rhames and we're live. The public has a right to know."

The SWAT commander gritted his teeth. "We got an active shooter on the top floor. We got two casualties we know of."

"Are they dead or alive?"

"Alive according to the last report. A woman cleaning offices saw two males both shot in the knee. She escaped down the emergency stairway before the shooter locked it down. He's jammed the elevator too."

"How many people are being held hostage?"

The commander gritted his teeth again. "Sit report is still coming in, but it appears everything is isolated to the top floor. Because of the late hour, the offices on the other floors were closed. Now let me do my job."

"One last question. What can you tell us about the shooter?"

"He's got a gun and he's not afraid to use it."

The commander signaled his heavily armed team to move out. Jack held onto the mike boom and edged away from the news crew. He spotted a mobile command post and closed in on it. The door was open, but he stayed in the shadows to keep from being seen. Radios, telephones, and laptops crowded a table. Men and women crowded around that. Some were in uniform, some in plain clothes. Terry Dolan was in charge. He stood over a pair of twentysomethings wearing headsets and typing furiously.

"What do you have for me?" he said.

"We're in," the male twentysomething said. "We got ears."

"What about a mouth?"

"Only if he answers the phone when it rings."

"I'll do the talking then," said a plump man wearing a blue nylon Windbreaker with the words *Police Negotiator* printed in dayglow letters.

Terry said, "What about eyes? Where are we with that?"

The female twentysomething was chewing gum as she typed. "Still working on it. It's an old building. It doesn't have Nest, can you believe it? And the CCTV system is as old as a landline. It isn't even connected to the cloud so hacking's a real bitch." She blew a bubble and it popped.

"Phone's ringing," her fellow tech said.

"Pick it up. Go ahead, pick it up," Terry urged.

"Bingo. We got a connection," the male tech said. "I'll put it on speaker."

The negotiator took his seat. He opened and closed his mouth a few times like a singer stretching his jaw for a concert. "Good evening. My name is Bill Chae. I work for the police department, but I'm not a cop. Who am I speaking with?"

The only answer was a series of clicks and the sound of chopper blades thwap-thwapping over the building.

"Okay," Chae said, "I'll start off. First, I'm here to help. Is there anything we can get you? Water, food, cigarettes?"

Still no answer.

"If you want anything, just ask. I hope we can agree that we all want the same thing. A peaceful end to this situation so everyone can go home safe. What do you say?"

The speaker cackled with coughing. Jack tensed. And then the voice confirmed it.

"I already got some of what I want," Benicio Tuxtla said. "Can you give me the rest?"

"That depends, sir. What should I call you?"

"Ocho."

"Is that a first name or last?"

"You choose."

"Okay, Mr. Ocho. What is it you still want?"

"I want the man who owns this building sent up. Frank Penny."

Terry stiffened and then twirled his fingers and whispered to a uninformed cop who was standing beside him. "Find out where Penny is at and get him over here fast. Maybe he's this guy's boss. Maybe this guy is a sore customer. We may need to put Penny on the phone to get him to put down his gun."

Chae kept speaking in a calm and encouraging manner. "Okay, Mr. Ocho, we'll see what we can do about that. Now, you said you already got some of what you wanted. May I ask what that was?"

"I got a punk here who works for Penny. I'll trade him for Penny."

"And what is the individual's name, sir?"

"Go ahead and tell him," Tuxtla growled.

"It's Ricky Udo and he's crazy. Duct taped me to a chair. Got a gun on me. Give him whatever he wants or he's going to shoot me. He's—"

The sound a steak makes hitting the butcher's counter came across the speaker. "Shut up, punk."

Chae said, "Please, Mr. Ocho. Can we agree to no violence, please?"

"He ain't hurt, but he may need a change of underwear." Tuxtla coughed. "You got Penny on his way up yet?"

"We're still trying to locate him. How many other people are there with you?"

"I don't count so good."

"How about if we agree that for trying to locate Mr. Penny, you let the people there go?"

"Forget it."

Chae leaned toward the mike. "I understand a couple of people are in need of medical attention. Let's at least agree to let the paramedics come up and take them back down in exchange for us bringing Mr. Penny here."

"I don't need to do shit. Send Penny up or more people going need a doctor, starting with him."

Udo screamed.

"But, sir, we must be able to treat the injured—"

"The pair I clipped are Penny's muscle. Getting shot goes with the paycheck."

"Let's agree that no one else will get shot."

"Sure." Tuxtla coughed. And then he spit. "Don't mean I won't throw them out the window though."

"Sir," Chae said quickly. "The police won't agree to let you speak with Mr. Penny if you threaten violence."

Tuxtla's laugh turned into a cough. "Who said anything about speaking to him? Killing him is more like it. Kill him like I did his rotten kid. Rid this city of their bloodsucking kind."

Terry signaled the tech to put it on mute. "Did he just admit to killing Frank Penny Jr.?"

"Sounded that way to me," the uninformed cop standing

next to him said.

Terry motioned to Chae. "Go ahead and ask him. The tape's rolling." He signaled the tech to take it off mute.

Chae leaned in again. "I don't believe I heard you correctly, Mr. Ocho. What did you say about Mr. Penny's son?"

"You forget to clean your ears this morning? I said I caught that little punk in an alley one night and gave him what he had coming. Beat his ass into the ground. Got away with it too. Dumb cops chased some taggers down the alley while I walked free. Now, where's his old man at? He's the one I want. Pay back for the way he's been ripping everybody off."

"And I thought my landlord was screwing me," the uniformed cop muttered.

Chae said, "I'm sorry, Mr. Ocho, but we're still trying to locate Mr. Penny. You'll have to give us more time. While we wait, how about we talk about the people in the building again. Show good faith and let some of them go."

"Think I'm stupid?" Tuxtla shouted. "Quit jerking me around and send up Penny or people going start flying out the window. Starting with this *güero* here."

Udo's scream made the speaker reverberate.

Terry gestured at the tech to put it on mute again and said to Chae, "How much longer do you think you can keep him on?"

Chae grimaced. "All the signs are pointing to him breaking it off."

The detective nodded and then toggled his radio. "This is Dolan. Give me SWAT Leader One." Terry waited. "Commander, the shooter is threatening to throw people out the window. We know he's in the room with at least three hostages, but there could be more." He listened. "How's your team making out? Okay, we'll keep him talking while they work on breaching the fire door. What's that? Understood. But only if you get a clear shot."

Jack let the mike boom fall to the ground. He thought of entering the mobile command center. He thought of turning around and going back home. But he did neither. Once again, the Latin lessons drummed into him at St. Joseph's echoed. *Alea iacta est.* Julius Caesar had said it when he marched on Rome: *The die is cast.*

Chae started speaking again. The negotiator was still using a calm voice and trying to sound empathetic. He was careful not to ask yes or no questions, level any judgement, or make promises.

Mobile spotlights that had been wheeled into position switched on simultaneously. Their powerful beams bathed the building in bright white light. The helicopter circled lower. Jack heard a panicky shout over the speaker.

"Get your hands off me!" It was Ricky Udo.

Jack looked up at the top floor of the building. A spotlight was trained on every window. Two pistol shots echoed and glass exploded outward from a floor-to-ceiling window. A man's figure seated in an office chair filled the open frame.

"Don't shoot! I'm a hostage!" Udo yelled.

And then the chair rolled forward and Udo's scream followed him all the way down to the cement sidewalk eight stories below. Jack couldn't take his eyes off the blown-out window. Another figure filled it.

Benicio Tuxtla waved a gun and yelled, "I'm ready!"

He fired into the night sky. A fusillade of high-powered rifle shots answered, blowing him backwards.

"Suspect down! Suspect down!" a voice shouted over a dozen radios. "Go! Go! Go!"

But Jack was no longer listening. He knew what they would find on the floor of Frank Penny Sr.'s office. A dead man no longer walking.

## 36

The breakfast plate was piled high. Two sunny-sides rode atop a sea of refried beans. Links of chorizo surrounded it like a barrier reef. Side dishes brimmed with fresh guacamole, red sauce, green sauce, and fried bananas. A basket overflowed with handmade flour tortillas freckled to perfection. Jack knew he couldn't finish even half of it, but he gave it his best. *Abuelita* beamed from the kitchen. Every so often she would cross herself, clasp her hands, and say a silent prayer of thanks.

He was working on a *café con leche* when Terry Dolan entered the restaurant and sat down at the table.

Jack said, "I wouldn't have guessed you owned a polo shirt, much less wear one on a workday. The department must be relaxing the dress code. Help yourself to a tortilla."

"I hear they're going to release Hark any day now," the cop said.

"That's what CB tells me. Some paperwork the State has to sign off on is all that stands in the way."

"Benicio Tuxtla's confession was well-timed, and the part

about the graffiti artists running away was particularly convincing."

Jack stirred a skin of hot milk floating atop his coffee and took a sip.

"The cleaning woman said Udo and two men seemed to be expecting him as if he'd called ahead and made an appointment," Terry said. "English isn't her first language, but she thought he was delivering something because Udo asked if he had it and Tuxtla said do you have the money. When Udo said yes, Tuxtla pulled out a gun and shot the two men in their knees and aimed it at Udo. That's when she ran out."

"Doesn't sound like it was about a mixed-up pizza order."

Terry frowned. "How well did you know him?"

"Who?"

"Don't play dumb. Benicio Tuxtla."

"Only what I learned about him watching the news. That Shauna Rhames is some go-getter. She'll get an Emmy nomination for sure." He pointed the mug at the cop. "What's with the change in wardrobe?"

"I looked into Tuxtla's record."

"The news said he was an ex-con. Spent most of his life at Folsom, right?"

"I mean beforehand. It turns out he grew up right here in the Mission. You didn't know him from back then?"

"Before my time."

"What about Hark?"

"What about him?"

"What's his connection to Tuxtla?"

"You'd have to ask him."

"Tuxtla got sent to Folsom on a murder charge. Before then, he ran a Mission District gang. *Los Guerreros*. On his rap sheet from way back then, there's mention of complaints filed by Frank Penny Sr. against Tuxtla and his boys."

"There you go. Don't you call that motive?"

"He harbors a nickel and dime loitering beef all the time he was behind bars?"

"I guess he had a lot of time to stew about it."

"Do you know when they performed the autopsy, anything that wasn't a bullet hole in his chest was a tumor. He was stage IV. It's why they commuted his sentence."

"Hey, I'm trying to digest my breakfast here. You didn't answer me. Where's your suit and tie?"

"If somebody wanted to, they could make a case for suicide by cop. And then there's Ricky Udo. Another convenience, considering you told me he killed Garza and Frank Jr." The detective leveled his stare at Jack. "Where's the gun you were going to give me?"

"See, if you played poker, you'd know a bluff when you saw one."

"Are you telling me you never had it? Why would you go to that kind of trouble?"

Jack finished the coffee. "And if you had a friend, you'd know you'd do anything to help him out of a jam."

"Anything?"

"Anything."

Terry's jaw tightened. "I finally got the lab reports back from Garza's shop. I got ballistics from the slugs they took out of his body, but no gun to match them to. They didn't match the one we found on Tuxtla nor another one we found in Penny's office. We assume Tuxtla took that one off of Udo or the two men he shot in the knee. I got the video tape from Garza's security camera all cleaned up so you can see through the spray paint. The trouble is, the two robbers were wearing masks and hoodies. You can't make out who they are."

"That's too bad. Now you still have an unsolved case."

"The only thing you can see is they both shot him. The first robber shoots twice. The robbers have an argument. There's no sound so you can't hear what they're saying. But then the second robber takes the gun and shoots Garza in the head to make sure."

"Maybe I made a lucky guess. Maybe one of them was Udo."

"Maybe."

"Is that why you're dressed to spend your days in the backyard? Did brass put you on leave until after the election's over because the Penny killing solved itself but Garza's remains open?"

"You think you're so smart."

"I get it. The department's calling it a vacation. Where are you going?"

Terry paused. "It's not a forced leave. I'm taking some personal time."

"Really, what for? To get in touch with the real you? Katie would tell you that's good. She's got the kids doing yoga and me meditation. Sometimes it even works." Jack put his napkin on the table. "How long you gone for?"

"Indefinitely."

"You'll be back."

"I'm not so sure."

"Of course you will. The city's home. Your father was a cop. His father. It's in your bones. You're like me. We can't turn our backs on San Francisco no matter how hard people try and turn it into something it's not."

Terry stood. "If and when I do come back, I'm going to make it my business to look into the Garza case. You can count on it."

"I wouldn't expect anything else."

JACK WALKED over to the building where Benicio Tuxtla died and rode the elevator to the top floor. The receptionist ushered him into Frank Penny Sr.'s office. Workers had screwed plywood over the broken window and the carpet had already been replaced. The real estate baron sat behind his desk. Since he was always dressed for a burial, Jack couldn't tell if he was coming or going to one.

"I'm told you want to sell your building," Penny said.

"Business doesn't take a break for mourning?" Jack said.

"I am sure Father Bernardus and the nuns consider it a personal failure they were unable to cure you of your sacrilege. Fortunately for them, God will overlook their shortcomings."

"Does that include yours and your son's?"

Penny's throat bulged. "Let us make this conversation as brief as possible. Your message was you want to sell your building. Why now?"

"The crime around here is getting to be too much. First Garza, then your son, then right in here. Udo rides a chair out the window and his two pals go to the head of the line for knee replacement surgery." He mimed a shudder. "Makes you wonder about your own safety."

"You forgot to include the criminal responsible for all the carnage."

"I haven't forgotten about him. Far from it." Jack paused. "I brought along the blueprints to my building. Shall we take a look?"

Penny sighed. "If you think it makes any difference."

"I'm betting it will."

Jack opened the cardboard tube and extracted a printout of Better Tomorrow Capital's plans for Mission Street. He unrolled it on Penny's desk and stabbed his finger in the middle of the sheet.

"There it is. My little building."

Penny cleared his throat. It was all Jack could do to keep from looking around for a bullfrog croaking beneath the desk.

"Where did you get these?"

Jack ignored him. "Yep, there I am smack dab in the middle of all this planned development. I'd say I'm the linchpin to progress, wouldn't you? Oh, and there's a copy of BTC's prospectus listing partners and investors. You may have to polish your glasses because the point size is so small, but I take it FP&S is you."

Penny cleared his throat again. "I imagine you are operating under the assumption that this information means you are entitled to a higher sales price. Perhaps you're right."

"I'm right, all right. What will you give me for my building?"

Penny twiddled his thumbs. "What did you pay for it?"

"You know right down to the last penny." He smiled. "You also know what my carrying costs are as well as the cost of lost opportunity for having my capital tied up. And then there's the cost of giving up the possibility of riding the real estate boom even higher if I sell now. That's got to be worth a bundle. Okay, I'm easy. How about we fix a price that gives me a 400 percent gain."

"That's preposterous."

"Is it?"

"I tell you what. I will have my financial people run some scenarios. I'm sure we can reach an equitable accommodation."

"But wait. I almost forgot something." Jack whisked away the top page to reveal the same blueprint marked up with red ink and notes.

"What is this?" Penny's eyes bulged behind his thick glasses.

"It's what is really going to be built there. See where the old movie theater is where you guys were planning a high-rise? Forget it. It's going to be renovated into a community theater and performing arts space. Those dotted lines along the side indicate classrooms and studios. And this? Where you had it marked for high-end condos? Forget about those too. You're going to build rent-subsidized affordable housing for families. Cicero Broadshank's firm is drawing up an ironclad provision for the City to make sure it's enforced."

"Have you lost your mind?"

"And all the existing shops and restaurants along the street stay, but they get free facelifts and stabilized leases. Here's the pièce de résistance. The endcap, that old abandoned gas station you own that's been leaking for decades? The tanks get yanked, the soil cleaned up, and the lot turned into a public park with swings. A slide too. I've always liked a slide."

Penny's face turned as red as his leather furniture. "Get out of my office immediately."

"Wait. I got one more document." Jack turned the page to reveal an enlarged photograph of a gun. "I took this off your boy Ricky Udo. See those splotches? That's fingerprint dust. Guess what? They're a dead bang match for Udo's and Frankie's too. But wait, wait. It's like the late-night shopping channel. There's more. A lot more. A friend who is a wonder getting stuff brought me a copy of a ballistics report from an evidence box at SFPD. Guess what? The rifling on the slugs they took out of Garza is a match to this gun. Seems Frankie and Udo both used it to shoot Garza. Frankie first out of panic, Udo second to make sure."

Penny sputtered and then got control of himself. He clasped his hands together and bowed piously. "Clearly, my poor son must have succumbed to temptation and strayed from the path of righteousness. A criminal confessed to his murder and so my son paid dearly for his sins. The Lord works in mysterious ways."

"Clearly." Jack gave it a few beats. "Except for one thing."

"And what is that?"

"The night Udo and his Raiderettes jumped me outside my

office? I had the ultimate butt dial when I hit the sidewalk. My phone called my own voice mail and left a recorded message. Only it wasn't me talking, it was Udo bragging how you ordered him to kill Frankie to keep his mouth shut."

"How dare you?" Penny croaked. "You're the devil."

Jack pulled out his phone and held it up. "Let's see who really is."

"You're bluffing. You don't have any such recording."

"One way to find out." Jack started clicking the display. "Did you know you can forward voicemails? Now, what's the number for Robbery Homicide again?"

"Even if you do have one, it proves nothing. It would be the word of a dead man versus mine, and may I remind you of who I am."

"Oh, I know who you are. I know exactly who and what you are. I also know once I hit this button, it may not get you arrested, but you can forget about getting your calls returned from anyone at city hall, much less the diocese."

Penny crossed his arms. "Go ahead and send it."

Jack locked eyes with him. Penny returned the stare, but after a full minute, the nictitating membrane flickered.

"Wait!" Penny pushed both his hands out like stop signs. "This project you brought me. Maybe it does have some merit."

"Plenty, actually. You'll see it done?"

"What about the recording and gun?"

"They stay in the vault. Consider them collateral. For my health."

"I'll have to talk to my partners."

"I was hoping you'd say that. Give Supervisor Berlin a call right now. Tell him to meet me in Dolores Park in one hour."

"Why would he to do that?"

"He's got 2.7 million reasons why he'd rather hear from me about The Ethyl Rodgers Estate Trust than from his opponent."

## 37

S ome locals called the fog Karl. The spelling challenged thought it was in honor of the Sandburg poem with cat's feet or for a street in the Haight which often proved to be a climatic borderline. Jack knew it to be a Twitter creation promoted by a Tim Burton fan. Whatever the name's origin, it was a moot point because there was only blue sky and sunshine as he waited outside the gates of San Bruno Jail.

Hark strolled out at straight-up noon. He was wearing the same long-sleeved flannel shirt he had on the night he was arrested. The big man ran his hand appreciatively over the fender of his prized '64 Chevy Impala. Jack left it idling as he moved over to the shotgun bucket.

"Looks like Vinny buffed it out," Hark said as he slid behind the chrome chain-link steering wheel.

"Kid's going to hit you up for a raise, for sure. He's been punching a clock and keeping track of overtime while you were away."

Hark gave the accelerator a few taps and listened to the Flowmasters growl. "Nice. Where to, *vato*?"

"How about the ballpark? Game time is in an hour. Giants and Dodgers. Katie's holding a couple of seats for us."

"Why didn't you say so? Let's jet."

He hit the gas and the low-slung sedan hugged the asphalt as they cruised toward downtown.

Hark said, "Broadshank gave me the lowdown on what went down that got me sprung. That dude Tuxtla sure solved a lot of problems."

Jack watched the scenery pass by.

"I got a look at him at the prelim," Hark continued. "He doesn't resemble me at all. So why'd he do it? He didn't owe me nothing."

"Maybe he did it for himself."

"Whatever his reason, what he did?" Hark pounded his chest. "Respect."

Jack could've sworn he'd just heard Tuxtla's gravelly voice.

They drove on. Hark said, "Vinny swung by yesterday. He got his dates screwed up and thought I was getting out. We visited some."

"He's got your back."

"He bragged about how he was in the thick of everything. Said he took a call from some dude in San Bruno who told Tuxtla it was Udo tried to take me out to protect his own ass."

Jack kept his eyes on the passing scenery.

Hark palmed the wheel as he drove one-handed. "Thing is, *vato*, I asked around the pen. You know, the *'manos* in *Nuestra Familia*. None of them knew what I was talking about. Didn't know nothing about any Aryan Brotherhood connection to a hit on me. Didn't know nothing about anybody calling Tuxtla from San Bruno."

They passed the Cow Palace. Jack remembered going to a rodeo there when he was a kid. His old man made him sit on the mechanical bull. Called him a pussy and gave him a smack when he got bucked off. Jack swore on the spot he wouldn't cry in front of him then or ever, promised himself if he ever saw his father smacking his mother again, he'd step right up and put a stop to it.

Hark shot a sideways glance at Jack. "Whoever made that call had brains and steel knowing it could set Tuxtla loose like it did. You know, with an ending like where those fat dudes and women are singing in Italian while everybody stabs everybody."

"You mean opera."

"Exactly. Those dudes."

"Pavarotti. Machiavelli."

Hark shook his head and then grinned. "Yeah, them too, *'mano*. Them too."

PREGAME ACTIVITIES WERE STILL on the field when Jack and Hark arrived at AT&T Park. Zita saw them first and ran up the aisle to greet them. She threw her arms around Hark's leg and called him *tio*.

"Look at you," he said, patting her on the top of her Giants hat. "Sporting the orange and black like a true faithful."

Katie was close behind. She handed Harry to Jack and hugged Hark, smothering his cheeks with kisses. She looped her arm through his and escorted him down to their seats right above the Giants' dugout.

Jack waited before following. He looked down at the field. A game was about to be played. There would be a winner and there would be a loser. There would be heroes and there would be goats. There could be injuries, some even career ending. The umpires would make calls; some would be correct, and others, mistakes. Baseball was like life itself. You never knew how it would turn out. And as Jack watched his family settle into their seats, he knew there were times when you had to put it all on the line for the good of your team. There would always be regrets for the things you did, but the trick was not to have them outweighed by regrets for not doing something when you had the chance.

He carried Harry down the steps to the row of orange plastic seats.

"You made it," he said to Sami Alfassi who was sitting with his son and daughter.

"Yes, thank you very much for the tickets," the shoe store owner said. "Your wife has been most kind explaining the rules to us. She gave Farid a baseball glove in case an errant ball comes this way."

"A foul." Jack said to the boy, "You catch it, you get to keep it."

Farid smiled.

The loudspeakers crackled as the announcer directed everyone to turn their attention to the pitcher's mound.

"Please welcome a special guest who will be throwing out the first pitch, Supervisor Erick Berlin."

The stands erupted with applause. Some fans stomped their feet so hard the rows of seats rocked.

Zita grabbed Jack's arm. "Is it an earthquake?"

"Don't worry, *mija*. It's only the fans having fun."

"There's never been an earthquake at a ball game before?"

Jack recalled the 1989 World Series when a big quake struck minutes before Game 3 between the Giants and A's. *Never say never,* he thought.

"It's okay. We're safe here."

She clapped her hands. "Goody."

Berlin was holding a baseball. He tossed it up and down a couple of times while he let the applause roll on.

"Thank you, thank you," he said into the mike. "It's an honor to be here. And it's an even greater honor to express a few heartfelt gratitudes. As you know, San Francisco has been through a lot the past couple of days, especially the Mission District. We owe a great many thanks to the proud men and women of the San Francisco Police Department whose selfless courage and tireless efforts help keep us safe." He paused as applause and cheers rocked the house again.

"I also want to give thanks to an outstanding citizen who suffered a tragic personal loss, Mr. Frank Penny Sr. I'm pleased to announce that Mr. Penny will be honoring his son's memory by partnering with the City to launch a redevelopment project on Mission Street that will feature new affordable housing reserved for low income families, a variety of cultural resources for the public, and a park. What's more, the project is earmarking funds to be used as grants to established small businesses in the corridor to help them stay and thrive."

Alfassi gave Jack a questioning look.

Jack shrugged. "The world works in mysterious ways."

"And, finally," the supervisor said. "I'd also like to give a special thank-you to a very generous anonymous benefactor who is donating $2.7 million to build and endow a center for immigrants and refugees. They have always been an important part of our social fabric and we need to do whatever it takes to make them feel right at home."

Hark said, "Man just punched his ticket to the mayor's chair and beyond."

As the applause mounted, Berlin shouted into the mike. "Thank you, San Francisco. Now let's play ball." And he toed the rubber, wound up, and threw a perfect strike.

"What got into him?" Katie said. "It's like he suddenly rediscovered his roots when he was a community organizer."

"Maybe he had a heart-to-heart with his dear old grandma Ethie," Jack said.

She arched a brow. "That would have been a very long-distance conversation."

Wonder Boy approached. He was carrying a thick, well-used baseball scorebook and three sharpened pencils.

"Did you hear about Miss S-S-Song?" the statistician asked.

Jack shook his head. "Did she pass her college exam?"

"She's on her way to Bangkok."

"Don't tell me she got deported? Broadshank told me he'd be able to help her with her visa."

"That will no longer be an issue. DD Mitchell is traveling with her. They are going to s-s-seek her mother's blessing."

Katie clapped. "Now that's what I call love."

"Cause for a celebration at least," Jack said. "I'll go get drinks. Anyone want a hot dog?"

Zita and Hark held up their hands. Sami Alfassi shook his head. "Alas, thank you, but our faith does not allow it."

"You're in luck. They got every kind of hot dog you can imagine. Besides pork, there's beef, chicken, turkey, even tofu. You name it, they got it. Don't want a dog? Then there's tacos, sushi, cooked crab, Thai, Italian, kebabs, and falafel. Don't get me started about garlic fries."

"So much variety," Alfassi said.

"Hey, this is San Francisco," Jack said. "It's the way we roll."

## A NOTE FROM THE AUTHOR

Thank you so much for reading *SHAKE CITY*. I'd truly appreciate it if you would please leave a review on Amazon and Goodreads. Your feedback not only helps me become a better storyteller, but you help other readers by blazing a trail and leaving markers for them to follow as they search for new stories.

To leave a review, go to the *SHAKE CITY* product page on Amazon, click "customer reviews" next to the stars below the title, click the "Write a customer review" button, and share your thoughts with other readers.

To quote John Cheever, "I can't write without a reader. It's precisely like a kiss—you can't do it alone."

## GET A FREE BOOK

Dwight Holing's genre-spanning work includes novels, short fiction, and nonfiction. His mystery and suspense thriller series include The Nick Drake Novels and The Jack McCoul Capers. The stories in his collections of literary short fiction have won awards, including the Arts & Letters Prize for Fiction. He has written and edited numerous nonfiction books on nature travel and conservation. He is married to a kick-ass environmental advocate; they have a daughter and son, and two dogs who'd rather swim than walk.

Sign up for his newsletter to get a free book and be the first to learn about his next novel as well as receive news about crime fiction and special deals.

Visit dwightholing.com/free-book. You can unsubscribe at any time.

# ALSO BY DWIGHT HOLING

**The Nick Drake Novels**

The Sorrow Hand (Book 1)

The Pity Heart (Book 2)

The Shaming Eyes (Book 3)

The Whisper Soul (Book 4)

**The Jack McCoul Capers**

A Boatload (Book 1)

Bad Karma (Book 2)

Baby Blue (Book 3)

Shake City (Book 4)

**Short Story Collections**

California Works

Over Our Heads Under Our Feet

Made in United States
Orlando, FL
27 April 2022

17203029R00150